E. d'Espérance

Northern Lights and Other Psychic Stories

E. d'Espérance

Northern Lights and Other Psychic Stories

ISBN/EAN: 9783337252359

Printed in Europe, USA, Canada, Australia, Japan

Cover: Foto ©Andreas Hilbeck / pixelio.de

More available books at **www.hansebooks.com**

NORTHERN LIGHTS

AND OTHER PSYCHIC STORIES

BY

E. D'ESPÉRANCE

AUTHOR OF "SHADOWLAND"

LONDON
GEORGE REDWAY
1899

TO

MY DEAR FRIENDS

MATTHEWS AND GRACE FIDLER

IN GRATEFUL RECOGNITION OF THEIR LIFELONG FRIENDSHIP

HELPFULNESS, AND SINCERE SYMPATHY

𝔗𝔥𝔦𝔰 𝔙𝔬𝔩𝔲𝔪𝔢

IS AFFECTIONATELY INSCRIBED

CONTENTS

PSYCHIC STORIES

INTRODUCTORY

ONE phase of thought, certainly by no means
modern, has played, and is playing, an important part in the lives and religious opinions
of a vast number of persons.   I allude to the
general belief among certain classes of simple
minded—I will not say ignorant—persons, of
the frequent return to earth of the departed,
and the intervention in human affairs of dis-
embodied spirits of men.

These beliefs are not confined to one country
nor to one people.   Nor can they be said to
exist among the most ignorant alone, for in
many cases the groundwork of these beliefs
defies the scientific investigator, who, armed
with learning, tries to explain them by the
natural laws with which he is acquainted.

My studies and investigations have been

more particularly in Scandinavia, in Bavaria,
in the Tyrol, and among the Wendish people
—the Sorber—that small remnant of a once
powerful Sclavonic race (now almost extinct)
which came from the East about the year A.D.
400. They inhabit a part of Saxony called
the Lauzitz district, although at one time they
were spread over an immense tract of country,
and traces of their language are left in such
names as Pomerania (*po more* = by the sea) ;
Leipzig (from *lipa* = the lind) ; Brietzen (from
breza = the birch). They are a somewhat
phlegmatic and unimaginative people, indus-
trious and thrifty to an extreme, in a country
where industry and thrift are the characteristic
features of the people. They are intelligent,
matter-of-fact, practical in all their actions,
deeply religious, and conservative in their
ideas, keeping strictly to all the observances
of church ceremonials, Saints' and holy days,
whether they belong to the Catholic or Luthe-
ran churches ; for, be it known, they are not
all agreed on questions of theology. Some of
the Wendish villages are peopled by adherents
to the Romish Church, and others exclusively
inhabited by the followers of Martin Luther.

However much they may differ in their religious opinions they are equally well informed, and agree entirely in the belief in the return of spirits, and their influence upon the living, as well as in the possession, by certain persons, of miraculous powers of healing, divination, or water finding. They are also great believers in the efficacy of charms for the protection of children, animals, or property, one of the most common of these being a red ribbon, tied round the neck or wrist of a fine, well-grown, healthy child, or round the neck or tail of an animal that is either a favourite with its owner or is a particularly fine creature—the red ribbon being supposed to ward off evil powers in much the same way, presumably, as anything of a red colour has a deterring effect against the onslaughts of certain birds and animals. It is to be remarked that a puny child, or an animal of average, or under average quality, is not supposed to be the object of envy by the supernatural powers, and in that case the same precautions are not taken. On the same principle it is dangerous to remark on the thriving appearance of either child or animal, lest the hidden powers should hear and act upon it to its disadvantage. Therefore it is customary, when admiration of any living creature is expressed, to quickly add the words, " Let it be as though unspoken."

Another charm, not quite so innocent, is one curative of diseases of the skin. Any one so afflicted, they say, need only bury a garment which he has worn next the body. This garment, if discovered by any person or animal, transfers the disease from the one who wore the garment to the finder thereof. This custom is so common—being said to be a positive cure—that the authorities inflict a penalty on any one found to have buried such a garment, though, to avoid discovery, it is usual to tear it into shreds and bury it piecemeal. Many sicknesses among dogs are supposed to have been traced to the digging up of such disease-laden rags.

Among these same people are certain individuals said to be able to cure diseases by the simple process of " speaking over " the sick persons. The efficacy of the operation in two separate cases can be vouched for, as these cases occurred in the household where

I was residing. One patient—the cook—
had been incapacitated for some weeks, and
the doctor who attended her comforted her
by saying it was only a matter of time, she
must be patient. She, however, could not
be patient, and one evening sought the wise
woman of the village—a crone of nearly a
hundred years—and returned apparently quite
cured, telling delightedly of her restored
health, and at the same time asking permission to attend a ball, to be given in a day
or two's time. There did not seem to be any
mistake as to the woman's previous ailments,
nor could there be any mistake as to her
apparent restoration to health. But how was
it done? The young woman was obstinately
silent as to the words used or means em-
ployed by the healer. That was a secret she
might not reveal, she said.

Another case was that of the gardener, who
was suffering from rheumatism and swollen
joints. His cure was not so rapid. He was
obliged to pay three visits to the same wise
woman; nevertheless the cure was completed
within ten days.

Another method of healing practised by

men on their own sex, is that of "pulling."
The patient is stretched on the ground, his
body twisted, and his limbs pulled till they
accord with measurements taken by the
"doctor" while the patient was in good
health. This method is, they say, singularly
successful with many diseases. If the patient
is not cured it is generally asserted that
it is because the "doctor has lost or
forgotten his measurements." From the
reports of the patients themselves this process of cure is not without certain draw-
backs; for, if cured of his maladies, he
comes out of the struggle with a distinct
sensation of soreness, and a few blue or
black marks on his body.

The "Water Finder" is a man much in
request. One whom I have met in the
exercise of his calling interested me greatly.
He was of the peasant class, yet superior to
the ordinary type, with quiet, refined man-
ners, low voiced and slow of speech, and
having a somewhat abstracted and slightly
melancholy look about the eyes, that now
and again gave place to a startled expression
when he was spoken to. I followed him for

a couple of hours one morning, noting his movements, as he walked slowly along carrying a forked willow twig in his hands. It was a question whether there was water to fill some new fish ponds that were about to be made, and the services of the Water Finder were engaged to find out, first, if there was water to be had, and, second, where, and at what depths. Grasping a prong of the forked twig λ in each hand, holding it upright, the apex pointing to the skies, the man walked slowly onward in a zigzag direction, followed by several curious and interested onlookers. After a time the twig writhed like a living thing in his hands, and bent over outwards till the apex pointed to the earth.

"Here is water," he remarked quietly. "Mark the place."

"How deep?" asked the forester, who walked by his side.

"Thirty feet at least!"

"Too deep! Go on."

A little later the same writhing of the twig occurred, and again it pointed downwards.

"Here is also water. Mark the place!"

" How deep think you ? "

" Ten feet about."

Again and again the performance was repeated, the Water Finder giving instructions that the places should be marked, and stating the depth at which water would be found.

In answer to inquiries as to how he knew of the depth, he replied that it was only by experience, and that he had learned to judge of the distance of the water. The nearer the surface, he said, the more like a living thing did the twig act. Indeed it sometimes blistered or broke the skin of his hands, in twisting itself downwards.

" What do you suppose is the reason of its acting in this manner ? " he was asked.

" I cannot tell. It is, I suppose, the life that is in the twig that longs for water, and tries to reach it. The twig must be cut from a branch that grows beside and overhangs water, and it must only have been cut a few hours ; it must be thirsty, but not dried and withered, or it will not act."

" But if left to itself it would lie and

wither; water would have no power to draw it nearer to it?"

"No! there must be something in my hands which helps it, but I do not understand it. There are so many things we cannot understand!"

Among the party who accompanied the Water Finder there were several who held the twig as directed, but in every case except one, that of a lady, the twig remained perfectly passive. With the lady, however, the twig became quite lively when she came near the indicated spots; and when she carried it towards a pond of water, it wrenched itself with such force that it caused an abrasion of the skin on the lady's palms.

Boring later at the marked spots, the fact was proved that water existed there and at or about the indicated depths. From the supply of water obtained from the springs found by the Water Finder, on that occasion, a miniature lake of 2500 feet long, by 800 or 900 feet broad, has been filled, as well as a fish pond of nearly double that area.

There are to be found also certain persons gifted with the power of stemming the flow of blood from wounds. Many cases are related where accidents, to men or animals, appeared likely to result in death from loss of blood had it not been for the timely arrival of the "Blood Stopper," who, by touching the open wound, or passing his hand over the veins, caused instant cessation of the flow of blood.

These wonders are not believed in and practised by the peasant class alone. The services of the "Water Finder" and "Blood Stopper" are sought by all, whether high or low. Indeed, a certain nobleman at the Court is said to possess the water-finding power in a high degree, and is not above practising it when required.

Under these circumstances, in a district where miracles such as described are of daily occurrence, one can scarcely wonder that the people are firm believers in supernatural influences, ghosts, and haunted houses or localities.

The up-to-date materialist would say that it is only in such a hot-bed of superstition that ghosts can thrive, and that the miracles can be explained by natural laws; that, in point of fact, the miracles could not be performed among persons of more enlightened and scientifically trained minds; that, given a few ignorant villagers, a modicum of faith, rather more than a modicum of credulity, together with one or two knaves to cunningly mix the whole, miracles and ghosts could be produced *ad libitum*.

Spiritualists would say, on the contrary, that the simple lives, the simple faith, and religious instincts of the people bring them nearer to the great unseen world of spirits; and that their minds not being hampered or biassed by sceptical or materialistic ideas, the spiritual influences have a fair field for their operations.

Be this as it may, it is not my province to assert the one or the other, but only to relate facts, and leave the reader to judge which is the more reasonable conclusion. One remark, however, I must add. It is hard to see what part ignorance, faith, credulity, or cunning can play in the actions of a willow twig, or in the sudden cessation of the flow of blood from the cut arteries of a horse.

It is true that the belief in ghostly visitants can have at times very unpleasant results, and one is inclined to anathematise the overween-

ing credulity which caused them.   I will relate
one case in point, where this belief was the
cause of a serious loss and the escape of some
daring burglars.

The home of a friend of mine in the same
district was one night entered by burglars.
They made their entrance—as was discovered
too late—through one of the second floor
windows by means of a ladder.   The whole
of that floor was unoccupied at night, save
one little room in which a man-servant slept.
On the floor above were the sleeping rooms
of the family, and one or two maids.   On the
floor below—the ground floor—the watchman
and the dogs were supposed to keep guard.
On the following morning the robbery was
discovered.   A quantity of jewellery, plate,
and valuables was missing, and, as if to show
how leisurely the thieves had prosecuted
their search, they had chosen, and evidently
lighted, some choice cigars, and had also
emptied a bottle of wine.

On comparing notes, it turned out that
every one in the house had heard sounds of
footsteps, of doors opening, and of low voices
in conversation, but such sounds being usual,

no one had thought it worth while to get out of bed to investigate matters.

"Of course I heard something moving about," said the lady of the house, "but that is so often to be heard that, if I disturbed myself every time, I should never get a night's rest."

The night watchman, an old retainer of the family, remorsefully confessed that he had heard the sounds, and that the dogs had barked and growled for some time. "But," he added, "I quietened them so as not to disturb anybody, because of course I naturally thought that it was the old baron or some of the other ghosts that always walk about the castle at nights."

The servant who slept near to the rooms which had been the scene of the robbery confessed to having been aroused by sounds of whispering and by hearing the dogs bark; but he, too, concluded it could only be the ghosts a little more in evidence than usual, and crossed himself piously, praying that they might not come near him.

So the burglars got clear away with their booty and were never traced.

Though, according to report, "the old baron and other ghosts" continue to perambulate the castle rooms, the barred shutters that have since been provided to all the accessible windows, and the electric bells communicating with various departments of the household, that have been arranged in every room, have afforded protection against nonghostly or burglariously-minded intruders.

It was my residence in this castle, and association with the people in the vicinity, that suggested to me the idea of collecting the various stories, and presenting them to the public. Those contained in this volume are but a very small part of what have been related to me. I have chosen them because, in all cases where I have not myself participated in the recorded incidents, the narrators are known to me, as well as to hundreds of other people, as being both trustworthy and veracious. Where names have been used in the stories, they are the actual names of the people and places. When initials only have been used, it is because the persons most concerned are either still living themselves, or their near relatives are still on earth, and object to having any clue to their identity given to the public.

In most cases, where it has been practicable, these stories have, moreover, been submitted to the actors therein or the narrators thereof, in order that no inaccuracy might inadvertently be published.

"AGREED. I'll pay you sixty kronas a week for horse, sledge, and your services, all included. You understand?"

"Yes," said the peasant, "I'll drive you round by Haparanda, or across the Gulf on the ice, if you care to venture it. This grey mare goes like the wind. I got her cheap, because she has run away more than once."

"Ja så! That's not much of a recommendation," said Herr Massie, regarding the beautiful animal, who looked round as if interested in the bargain that was being made. "However," continued the gentleman, "my nerves have carried me through worse things than a drive after a runaway horse, and when one knows what to expect one can keep a tight hand on the reins."

This conversation took place outside a little hostelry in Norrland, in the north of

Sweden, one bitterly cold winter's day. The traveller who was engaging the peasant, as well as horse and sledge for a long journey, knew the country well, and had purposely chosen this season for his visits to the remote northern districts, on account of the greater facility which the frozen lakes offered for short cuts, and for the greater comfort of travelling by sledge compared with the primitive cariole.

The bargain concluded, the Bonde, as is the custom of his class, came forward with another stipulation—which as a rule is one of the greatest importance to the contracting party though seemingly an afterthought.

"Well, what is it?" said Herr Massie, seeing the inevitable request in the man's manner.

"It is nothing particular, only I can't engage to drive you after eight o'clock in the districts where Knifven, Rosén, and those rascals, shorten a fellow's shadow for him, or past the house they are known to frequent. People say there are so many ghosts there —ghosts of those they have robbed and murdered."

"It appears to me I'm in for a lively journey," remarked Herr Massie with a shrug of the shoulders. "However, I'm not afraid of ghosts nor of the cut-throats either for that matter. In any case I'll try to arrange that we pass their hospitable dwelling before dark."

This was easier said than done, for it sometimes happened that ten o'clock struck before they seated themselves, well wrapped in furs, behind the restive, excitable horse, and in the short day of four or five hours they were frequently unable to reach the next stopping place.

They had passed through the district said to be infested by the dreaded thieves and still more dreaded ghosts, without encountering either the one or the other, although a little incident had occurred which terrified Petter not a little. He had allowed the mare to have her head, and she, nothing loath, had as he said "flown like the wind." Coming to a sharp curve the sledge overturned, and both Herr Massie and he were thrown down the steep bank, against the very walls of the house they had been so anxious to avoid.

Herr Massie had struck with such violence against the fence, that he needed Petter's help to climb back to the roadway and regain his seat. Fortunately his hurts were not serious, for Petter, half dead with fear, could not be induced to linger in the neighbourhood a moment longer than was necessary to get his master bundled into the sledge, and the furs thrown in beside him ; and urging his horse to its utmost speed, he did not check its pace till they had left the danger far behind.

During the long journeys the Bonde regaled Herr Massie with all the gruesome stories, current in these northern latitudes, of ghosts, spirits of the unburied, who, dying in the winter, must wait till the breaking up of the frosts in the hard iron-like ground for their bodies to be placed under the sod, and in the meantime they, the ghosts, must wander mournfully about in the vicinity of their old haunts.

On one bitterly cold day, Herr Massie, anxious to reach a certain hostelry, announced his intention of attempting to cross a lake which would shorten the distance by a couple of hours. The cold had come suddenly, and Petter questioned whether the ice would bear; "but," as he remarked, "the first ice is always strongest," and it was a good distance to save. The Swedish peasant is wont to say that if he throws his glove on the ice without its breaking through it will bear him; and, if it will bear his axe thrown upon it, it is safe for his horse and sledge.

Petter therefore turned his horse's head towards the broad sheet of water covered with a thin coating of ice that looked black in the gathering dusk. Once or twice the mare was about to venture on to the dark surface; but either it was mistaken for water or she considered it unsafe, for she required a good deal of urging and encouragement before she could be induced to leave the strand. Once on the ice it was evident the horse was wiser than her masters, for great white cracks began to run out from the sledge and the horse's feet as she plunged forward in nervous fear.

Herr Massie quietly unbuttoned his coat, to be ready for a swim for life. Petter held the reins loosely, encouraging the frightened animal to its utmost speed. The silence and loneliness, the weird light from the northern skies, the uncertainty of life or death over-powered the two men who, with the exception of a word now and again to the horse, sat still without speaking. Their thoughts, whilst concentrated on the opposite shore, also fled to their homes and friends, wonder-ing too a little, if they did not reach land in safety, whether their fate would ever be known.

To say the horse went like the wind would be no exaggeration, for it was wild with terror. At last they neared the thicker ice unworn by undercurrents, and the two men drew a long breath as the beautiful creature landed them safely on *terra firma*. Nor was it till the danger was over that Herr Massie felt how great a strain it had been on his own nerves.

" Thank God, that is over," he said, patting the trembling animal. "We have you to thank, too, my lass, for your speed was our safety."

They reached the hostelry without further

adventure, and rose next morning with the intention of proceeding on their way as soon as they could get ready. But during the night, the most intense cold had set in. Herr Massie left his room, and running across the snow-covered lawn found the snow crackled harshly under his feet; his face and hands felt as though stung by nettles; and a burning sensation in his throat made him gasp for breath. He stopped for a moment, surprised to find that his nostrils closed, and he wondered what was the matter. Every movement seemed to make a rattling metallic sound in the air, as though he were forcing his way through some substance, displacing its atoms which closed again behind him.

He looked at a thermometer that hung on a wall. No quicksilver was to be seen. He crossed to the stables where he saw another. His curiosity induced him to break it, and he found the quicksilver in it in a frozen condition, showing that the frost was over 40 degrees below zero.

Most of the guests at the inn decided to remain there that day, and settled down to the usual occupation of belated travellers in these regions, namely, card playing and drinking.

Herr Massie, who represented an English firm that exacted full value for all outlays, decided to push on. Three or four of his predecessors had been lost; one was found dead in a boat, another was drowned, and the rest had disappeared somewhat mysteriously.

The horse was soon ready, but they had not driven a mile when the driver's face was frost-bitten, and they had to stop to rub it with snow. They set off again, but the day seemed full of trouble and difficulties. At length Petter said, "I must give it up; I cannot go any further."

They had reached Dufved, and it being Saturday, it was arranged to put up there.

Restless and energetic, Herr Massie decided that, as he was in any case prevented by the intervention of a Sunday from doing any business for a couple of days, he would make a holiday.

Obtaining a pair of snow skates (Skidor) and engaging a guide, the two set off for Mullfjell, one of the mountains on the northern Swedish-Norwegian frontier. They

had two or three hours before the setting of
the sun, and had covered several miles. The
cold was still intense, but the rapid pace had
prevented their feeling it, protected as they
were by furs. As the sun went down, they
came to the Kota of some Lapps who were
herding their reindeer on the mountain.

Besides these herdsmen, their dogs and
their deer, no living beings were to be seen
for many miles around. Herr Massie, beginning to feel somewhat tired, resolved to ask
their hospitality and shelter for an hour or
two.

"Come in," said one of the Lapps. "The
dogs will not bite; you need not be afraid."

Herr Massie bent his head and crept into
the Kota—a kind of wigwam built of poles
placed upright in a circle, leaning towards the
centre, which is left open at the top to allow
the smoke from the fire, which is directly
under it, to escape. The fire itself takes up
some three or four square feet in the centre
of the hut, so that men, women, children, or
dogs must lie or sit round about. There is
not much room for visitors.

"You look tired," said the Lapp who had

invited Herr Massie in. "Will you eat some dinner with us? We have not much to offer you, but if you can take such as we have you are very welcome. Lie down and make yourself comfortable on those pine twigs."

Herr Massie accepted both invitations, and stretched himself on the springy couch of pine branches. There was not height enough to sit comfortably, except close into the neighbourhood of the blazing fire, that every now and then filled the Kota with smoke; but Herr Massie was quite content to eat his dinner in a recumbent position.

"Can you not eat the meat?" asked the Lapp. "Put your hand behind you, and you will find some beef; pull it out. There's the hatchet, chop a bit off and roast it; it's more tasty than the boiled."

Massie did his best to make a meal of the roasted and boiled meat, to which were added some small potatoes about the size of marbles. Then his host poured out for him a cup of coffee, into which he put a spoonful of sugar and another of salt. "Do you like milk in it?"

Massie nodded. He felt a little dubious about the mixture, but he did not wish to hurt the feelings of his hospitable host.

A young man or woman—Herr Massie could not distinguish from the dress which it was—took from under the ends of the pine trees that formed the Kota the stomach of a reindeer, which was filled with frozen milk. A lump was chopped off and dropped into the coffee, which Massie courageously tried to swallow. Finding, however, that it was likely to act as an emetic, he quietly emptied the cup into the ashes of the fire.

"Then you've been in England, I suppose?" remarked the Lapp; "and you'll know the Prince of Wales. He bought some reindeer from us, but that was before the terrible storm when we lost so many. Poor Karin was amongst us then. I was to have been married to Karin, but she preferred little Napoleon, and I did not care for any other girl, so I never took a wife, and now I'm nearly sixty. No! I'll never marry now. You'll stay with us to-night, will you not? We've no beds such as you are likely to be accustomed to, but those pine twigs make a good enough bed when one gets used to them. You can have some reindeer skins, so you'll be warm enough. If you cannot sleep, you can watch the stars as they go past the top of the Kota. We are only seven, dogs and all included; so there's room."

Herr Massie thanked him for his kind offer, and accepted the invitation to spend the night among his new friends.

They asked him a hundred questions about France, Germany, and other countries, and when they had got all the latest news, they asked him to sing them a song, which Massie did to their great delight. Then the Lapps sang for him, and told him stories of their travels, till the evening darkened into night. Then they made a fresh pot of coffee, which Massie elected to take without the salt or chopped milk.

"I'm glad you came," said the patriarch of the family. "I never get to town now, to hear the news. The storm I mentioned, which ruined so many families of us, made a great change. I have never touched drink since. Karin and Napoleon made me feel that I never wanted to see the horrid stuff again. 'Who was Karin?' Why we were sort of cousins; her mother and my mother were half-cousins. I was very fond of her. You never saw such a pretty girl as Karin was, and she was as good as she was pretty. She had not the look of us Lapps, not red-haired nor black-haired, nor had high cheek bones as most of our girls have. No, she was fair and blue-eyed; her cheeks were round and red, her lips were always smiling, her face was the sweetest sight in the world to me. She was always working and always singing, as happy as the summer days are long. Yes, and when she married Nappi, it was as though the sun had gone down never to rise again. All was dark and dismal. Before that I saw the blue sippa in the woods, and the sweet-scented linnea that covered the glades; now I never see them. I used to hear the birds in the spring time and summer, but when I knew Karin was not for me I never saw nor heard them again. My heart has been heavy since then, and all the seasons are alike. The long months of summer's daylight or the months of

winter's night are all the same to me. Yes,
she was an angel, Karin was. Her children
grew up; still she was just as young to look
at as they, and they were so fond of her.
But the storm came and changed it all.
That was an awful misfortune. It happened
in this way. It had been bitterly cold, just
as it is now. Suddenly there was a change,
and it grew quite mild, and then began to
snow, and the snow fell in great soft flakes.
The wind rose too, and blew fearfully. Our
deer had no shelter, so they turned their heads
from the wind and stood still as they usually
do. But the snow kept falling—falling—
falling—all night and all day, and then in
the morning again it cleared up and began
to freeze as hard as it has done to-day. The
reindeer were all covered with a hard crust
of frozen snow, and they died from suffoca-
tion before we could get them out.

"'This was a terrible misfortune for Karin
and Nappi, as well as for many more. Their
boys and girls had to work for those who had
not lost all they possessed. Karin cried over
her troubles till she was ill. Nappi went to
Sundsvall and sold the few skins and things

they could spare, to buy medicine for her, but he bought brandy with the money and drank it himself. He only brought home a bottle of white brandy for Karin. This she drank, and after that she could never get enough. At last she and Nappi left us altogether, and I have never seen them since. They and their two reindeer were traced out to the main road. We heard they went southwards, begging their way from house to house, and were seldom sober, and that they often quarrelled. Then it was said that Nappi was dead, somewhere about Jerfso, where the people die of leprosy. I suppose that was the end of him. Others said he had been seen at Delsbo with the two reindeer, but that he sold them and bought drink with the money.

"When I heard he was dead, I went to look for Karin to bring her back to her people. I was away months at a time trying to find her. I often heard of an old Lapp woman begging for brandy and tobacco, and they said it must be Karin. But, you see, I was always thinking of the pretty blue-eyed Karin that I was so fond of, with her red cheeks and long fair hair; so when people told me they had seen a little, old, grey-haired Lapp gumma that was always drinking and smoking, I did not go to look for her; I could not think she was Karin.

"Afterwards, I was sorry I did not try to find the gumma, for I think if it had been Karin, I could have looked after her, and nursed her well again, and she would have been as good as she always was. I did once trace her to Delsbo, where some one said they had sold the deer to Knifven, but no one knew where she had gone, nor did any trouble themselves about any poor Lapps that were wandering about begging. I am always thinking about her, and whenever I meet strangers, I always ask if they have seen her. You that travel so much might some day meet her. If you do, will you try to send her here? I only want to look after her and help her to bear her troubles. No one else will do it. Tell me, will you help her if you meet her?"

"Certainly I shall," said Massie. "I once met an old woman running down the hill near Sollefteå. I had got out of my sledge to walk up the steep road, and was leading my horse, when she came down with a little sledge. I sat down on my sledge too. She stopped when we met, and knelt down on the snow and put her head on my knee, and began to cry. She asked me to buy her wedding ring. This is it I am wearing."

"That must be Karin's, it's just the same as she wore; yes! with thirteen little rings on it," said the Lapp, examining the peculiar ring which Massie showed on his finger. "What did she say to you? Tell me all you can."

"Well, you see, I never meet any of your people but I stop and talk to them, and this old woman seemed pleased to meet me. She gave me some grass that she said she had combed. It was about two feet long. I took off my fur boots, and she put some inside to keep my feet warm. I have always remembered her for that little gift. I have some of it still. I saw she had very little in her sledge, so I gave her a crown; and after she had rested, we parted and she went her way. I have not seen her since. It was several winters ago. Where she might sleep that night I do not know, and so little as

she had of warm clothing, poor woman, she
may have frozen to death, so cold as it was
just then."

Herr Massie did not find it easy to woo
the sleepy god, in spite of the bag of potatoes
which formed his pillow, and the reindeer
skins into which he rolled himself. A blazing wood fire made the Kota look warm,
but round about the walls the cold from the
ice and snow crept in, and cold gusts of
air seemed to drop down as the smoke
ascended and made its exit from the opening
in the centre of the roof. There was plenty
of ventilation in spite of the seven occupants
of the hut. Sometimes the smoke from the
fire spread itself throughout the Kota, which
Herr Massie's unaccustomed lungs resented.
If he turned his face to the fire his back felt
the tingling cold of the frost through the
pine stems. If he thawed his back by turning it towards the middle of the Kota, his
nose felt in danger of freezing.

After a while he rose and, stepping
softly over the dogs lying curled up near
the ashes, he opened the curtains of reindeer skins that covered the entrance of the

hut, and passed silently out into the frosty night.

A weird stillness lay over the earth; not a breath of air, not a sound! The stars shone with a hard glittering white brilliancy, scintillating in a sky of strange impenetrable blackness. The white mountains showed plainly against its darkness. The pine woods stood in sombre stateliness, their white snow plumes motionless in the frozen air. Not a movement, not a sound, broke the strange silence.

Then suddenly a faint glow flashed over the northern sky, spreading quicker than thought from east to west, deepening in brilliancy and unearthly radiance. Through the roseate glow flashed streaks of golden fire, waving like banners among dancing streams of crimson, green, blue, or glittering topaz. Brighter and brighter it grew, thrusting lance-like spears of ruddy flame towards the zenith; advancing, retreating, now paling into soft amber, now flashing into brilliant radiant light, rising higher, spreading wider, leaping over the northern heavens, till the sombre landscape, the white crested mountains, the dark pine forests, the snow covered plains were lighted up with its weird unearthly light. Separating itself from the earth it rose upwards, a mighty arch of lambent flame, the ends resting at the east and west, soft trailing garlands falling downwards like flowers to bind it with the darkened world.

Herr Massie stood spellbound. This wondrous spectacle held him motionless. It was no new sight, but here, in the undisputed kingdom of the frost king, the wide white world under the jewelled amethyst heavens, the stillness, the silence, the strange unreality struck him with a sense of the mightiness of the universe and the power which governs it, while the insignificance of human kind, with its thoughts, cares, and ambitions, seemed accentuated in the presence of this phenomenon of Nature.

"The bridge of the dead," said a voice behind him. Herr Massie turned to find his host at his shoulder.

"I saw you go out, and I followed you. It is not safe in this frost. Come in!"

"How do you mean? Why do you call it

the bridge of the dead?" asked Massie, still regarding the flaming arch.

"It is the bridge which the gods build, that the dead may come and go. Some are going to their home in Valhalla; some return to earth for a little space. When the bridge is built they crowd upon it, hurrying over. Old warriors with their horses, their swords and shields; one sees how they flash and glitter. Armies march over, with their flags and banners waving. The Lapps with their pulkas and their reindeer come back to scour once more over the frozen snow, and to warm themselves in the Kotas. Yes, the priests may say what they will. We Laplanders see many things of which the dwellers in houses know nothing. The old gods lived before the White Christ came, and they have not forgotten how to build their bridges, nor do the spirits of the dead forget the way over them. To-night they are coming and going in thousands. Listen, you will hear the clash of the swords —the tramp of hoofs—the crack of the whips. 'Tis the sound of the spirits hurrying, for the time is short and some have far to go."

The earnestness in the man's voice impressed Herr Massie in spite of himself, and as he watched the darting, waving streams of light, ever coming, ever going, and heard the faint detonations as the magnificent coruscations leaped in jewel-like brightness and splendour, casting their sparkling reflections on the gleaming snow, he thought it no wonder that the legends of the old gods lived still in the hearts of these children of the frozen North Land. They accepted the "White Christ," but the old gods were not dead.

As Massie covered himself again with the deer skins, and tried to settle his head more comfortably on his pillow of potatoes, he wondered to himself if the man really believed what he had said, or if his expressions had been but the outburst of poet nature, excited by the weird beauty of the strange scene.

The Lapp had spoken with an earnest enthusiasm that would imply belief.

He watched the man piling fresh logs on the fire. One could scarcely credit that under that ill-cared-for exterior, the brown, weather-beaten face, the small blue eyes that had grown used to peering through half closed wrinkled lids, the high cheek bones, the unkempt hair that fell in tangled straggling locks from under his old fur cap, there could dwell the heart of the poet. Yet as he remembered the story of the long weary search for the fair young girl who had long since become a wrinkled old woman, Herr Massie thought that there was no knowing the heart of man, for even that of a little old Lapp who had wandered the frozen wilds for sixty years held within it a spring of infinite love, pure and unselfish, and this being so, might not a poet's soul dwell beside it?

His speculations became vague and fantastic as he sank into dreamland, whence he was aroused by the stirring of his companions next morning.

When the time came for Massie to take his departure and make his way back to Dufved, where Petter awaited him, the Lapp offered to drive him in his pulka—the guide having left on the Saturday. The reindeer were harnessed and they set off, wrapped in skins, over the snowy wastes—a wild journey, but one the traveller enjoyed in spite of the probability of frequent upsets, as the flying steeds, encouraged by the voice, or the touch of the long whip, obeyed the rein which the Lapp threw from one side to the other of the antlered heads.

"You do not understand us Lapps," remarked the little man to Herr Massie, as they flew over the snow after the flying hoofs, "or I would tell you something which makes me now think Karin is dead. I am not quite sure, because I am always thinking about her, and when that is so it is not so easy to be sure. I have seen her so often in my dreams, just as she used to be when I hoped she would marry me, that it has been difficult to remember she had grown older. But sometimes lately it has been different. I have seen her every night, and heard her voice, and last night it was as though there could be no mistake, but I've been so weary and tired with waiting that I do not know what is real or what is my imagination."

"I do not know if I understand," replied Massie ; "I have heard a strange story that was told me by Petter, my driver ; it may interest you."

"What was that ?" eagerly asked the Lapp.

"When I was down South near to Ljusdal, Petter pointed out to me a little cow-house with a chimney, so that I could understand it was used as a dwelling in winter time for both cows and the people who owned them. Well, in that cow-house, it is said that there were the ghosts of two Lapps, an old man and woman. No one ever saw them except two little girls. The elder one about twelve years old said to her parents one day, 'There's an old Lapp and his woman outside, and they want some tobacco and brandy.' 'Tell them to go away,' said her mother, and looked out at the window to see what the beggars were like; 'I don't see any Lapps. Where are they?'

"'Over there beside the byre,' said Elsa, 'cannot you see them?'

"'No,' said her mother, 'there's no one there.'

"'Yes, there is,' said Mina, the other little sister, 'they are just going in at the door now.'

"This startled the mother and somewhat frightened her, because she saw the door open and close, and the fastenings on the outside

of the door could not be loosened by any one
inside. So she went out with her little girls
to try and understand what it was that was
going on. Just then the door opened and the
little girls said, 'There they are—cannot you
see them?'

"The mother rubbed her eyes and looked,
but no Lapps were to be seen. It was a sharp,
frosty, sunshiny morning, so she looked round
to see if any shadows from anything near
could make her little daughter mistaken; but
then the opening of the door—how was that
done? It was very strange, she said to herself,
as she nervously held Elsa by the hand.

"'I have no tobacco,' said Elsa, 'and
mother will not give me any.'

"'Who are you talking to?' asked her
mother.

"'To the old man,' said Elsa; 'do you
not see him standing there in the snow, and
his woman beside him?'

"She looked at the snow where Elsa
pointed, but there was not even a shadow to
mistake for a human being. Then Elsa said,
'You can have this if you like,' and held
out her hand in which she had a piece of

D

hard rye bread. As she did so, the bread quite disappeared.

"The mother began to get frightened, but she decided not to appear so to her little girls. 'I will shut and fasten the byre door —you better go in the house,' she said. Just then the door closed and fastened of itself; so she turned in a state of agitation and went into the house to think over what it could be and what she was to do.

"At noon the men came home from the woods, and she sent out the little girls until she told them what had taken place. .

"As soon as dinner was over they all went out, along with the little girls, to see the mysterious Lapps. Just as they did so, they saw the byre door open and shut and fasten of itself. Far went over to see who was behind the door, and the others kept watch outside. As he reached forward his hand to pull out the big wooden bolt, it came out of itself, and the door was flung open. This made him feel uncomfortable, but he went in and the door closed after him, and remained so until he was satisfied there was no one in the byre. When he went to the door, and was about to call to those outside to open it for him, it opened as though it knew what he wanted. All this was very strange, and every one except the little girls were more or less frightened. As soon as Far came out, the door closed and fastened.

"'Won't you give them some tobacco?' said Elsa; 'they are begging so for some.'

"'Of course I will. But where are they? I don't see them.' And he looked round with the tobacco in his hand.

"'Give it to me,' said Elsa; 'I will give it to them.' So she took the tobacco and held it out. All of them saw it, but how or where it went no one could say.

"'They want some brandy,' said Elsa; and Far, who was a steady, hard-working man, went into the house for the bottle from which he took a glass always before dinner. This he brought out, and filled a small glass which he held out to the mysterious Lapps. As long as he held it the glass remained full, but when he handed it to Elsa, and she held it out to her friends, it was quite impossible to see where the brandy went. That it went somewhere, and that the glass was emptied, no

one disputed.   When Elsa saw how surprised
they were, she and her sister took quite a
delight in giving away anything that was
handed them.

"The news rapidly spread abroad, and
many visitors came to witness the 'trick,' as
they called it, that the little girls had learned.
On Sundays there was quite a crowd to see
the 'conjuring,' and although the new-comers
saw the same as the father and mother, they
did not accept the fact as they saw it; they
said the little girls were very clever, and they
admitted all the facts except that of any old
Lapp or his 'woman,' as Elsa called her,
having anything to do with it.

"Soon after this the little girl Elsa caught
cold and was laid up with a fever, and during
this time the Lapps had evidently gone else-
where, as she did not see them again when
she got better."

"All that may appear strange to you,"
said the Lapp, "but to us it is not so. I
believe in the little girls, more than in those
who came to look on. I do not speak of
these things to people who live in houses,
for they do not understand them ; they laugh

at us, they say we are ignorant and uncivilised. They—the dwellers in houses and towns—may know some things better than we, but they are learned from books, and such learning is not real knowledge. They who write books may have learned to know, but those who only read what others know have no real knowledge of their own.

"They know how to lie and deceive; they know how to make the fiery spirit that they sell to the poor Lapps in exchange for deer and skins; they know how to make him drunk that they may make a good bargain, to send him away with brandy instead of meal or potatoes.

"They may know some good things too, I do not doubt; but it seems to me they have too much to think how to get richer than their neighbours, that there is no time to learn what is in the world except it concerns money. But we who live in tents, and wander about from one moss pasture to another, under God's free skies, learn much more. We are not afraid of our dead. We know they are with us. They come and visit us in our tents. We are glad to see them and bid them welcome, and are happier and better for knowing we have not lost them.

" Sometimes they wander about, miserable and wretched as those two poor souls of whom you speak.

" If I tell this to people who live in houses, they laugh and scoff, or they are afraid. I know it is because of their ignorance, and I excuse their rudeness, but I wish many times they knew as much of the reality of these things as we do, for then I think they would not, even for their own sakes, give our poor people the drink that ruins them while they live and keeps the poor souls wandering about wretched, ashamed, and miserable when they have died.

" It is this terrible drink that is causing our people to die out. Every year it is harder for us. We get poorer and fewer. In a hundred years I fear there will be none of us left. But even so, I would not exchange with the richest dweller in a house, if I must exchange my knowledge for his want of it in such matters as these which we have just discussed."

"BEN-NO-O! Ben-no-o-o!" Clear and shrill came the cry and was echoed from cliff to cliff, till the mountains themselves took it up in mocking mimicry, and derisively repeated "En-no-o-o-o!"

But there was no answer, except the twitter of a bird or the sound of trickling water.

"Ben-no-o-o!" Louder still, the mountains took it up again, and called in thunderous tones "Ben-no-o! En-no-o-o! No-o-o-o! O-o-o-o!"

There was no other sound to break the silence. The girl, who had made a trumpet of her hands, now shaded her eyes with them and glanced keenly about her. She gazed a little suspiciously at a clump of dwarf pine trees, some little distance to the left, and then, with a look of vexation, turned and re-entered the door of the Alm.

"A perfect young wretch," she muttered angrily; "it's the second time already, this week, he has served me the same trick."

"What has he done, my Cari?" asked the man, from the interior of the kitchen, where he was busy filling cartridges.

"Done! Just what he always does—let the cows stray out of hearing and then disappear himself, leaving me to find and drive them home alone."

"And just now you particularly wanted a quiet hour to talk to your sweetheart—is not that so?" he answered, laughing, putting his arm round her. "Well, let him go! I'll help to bring home the cows presently, if he does not come." So saying, he drew the girl from the open doorway, and they disappeared together into the cool shadow of the kitchen.

Outside the Alm the sun shone fiercely on the bare rocks that gleamed red and hot; except here and there, where the declining rays threw the shadow of some great boulder or jutting cliff, the heat was as intense as on an African desert. There was snow still on the higher peaks that stood sentinel-like above the Alm, but in the glare of the afternoon sun the very snow seemed to look hot.

Rising up eastward, a purple haze was spreading itself that might betoken a storm, but as yet it was far off, and in the meantime the heat, reflected as it was by the bare grey rocks, seemed almost suffocating.

A few minutes after the girl had disappeared inside the building, the clump of firs, which had seemed to attract her scrutiny, rustled a little curiously, seeing there was not a breath of wind stirring. Presently a bare, not over clean, leg wriggled itself into view, then another, till finally the whole form of a boy might have been seen lying flat on the ground. He listened cautiously for a moment; then, apparently satisfied that he was not observed by the girl or man, he slowly and noiselessly crept out of sight of the building, behind a boulder of rock. There he stopped, gazing fondly and admiringly on the rifle he had carried with him.

The hands and face of the boy might, from their appearance, never have made the acquaintance of soap and water, and the tangle of matted curly hair was only kept out of the glittering brown eyes by a ragged old felt hat, which sun and rain together had painted a nondescript colour that might once have been a green. The crown and brim had parted company in more than one place, but it was adorned by an eagle's plume, the boy's most valued treasure. Not that he was particularly dandified in his outward appearance, but he loved to excite envy and admiration in the breasts of the village boys, and met their inquiries as to where he obtained it with a discreet silence, only by various gestures and veiled hints leading them to imagine that a deed of valour and prowess was connected with the trophy.

Benno, the vagabond Benno, was the terror of all the mothers in the village, who feared for the morals of their offspring, but the delight of all the urchins, who considered him a most enviable creature, because he had no one to compel him to wash him-

self, comb his hair, or make himself otherwise respectable.

Benno, the vagabond, was a waif, who
came from nobody knew where, and belonged to no one. He had been found,
when an infant, in the church porch, wrapped
in an old horse blanket, and sucking con-
tentedly at a bottle of milk that was fastened
to the bundle.

Nobody knew where he had come from,
nor who had laid him there. There were
some ill-natured people who said that Räsl
at the inn could have told if she had
chosen to do so, but if she could, she
never did; so the infant was given to an
old woman to keep till something should
be found out about him. In the meantime the parish furnished the milk he drank,
and duly grumbled when it had to be
paid for.

After awhile he managed to crawl on
hands and knees, and then to toddle about
on two sturdy legs. Just then he began to
get into mischief, and from that time he
had never got out of it again. Benno was
no respecter of persons; he played his mis-

chievous pranks on all with a lofty disregard
of station or rank. From driving a team of
oxen a mile on the wrong road, while the
owner was inside the inn drinking beer and
joking with the girls, to driving a screw into
the jamb of the burgomaster's front door,
and compelling that worthy man to get out
of the window, no easy matter when one
considered the great amount of flesh he
carried and his shortness of breath, combined
with the very natural irritation he felt at
being obliged to adopt so undignified a
means of exit. From tickling trout in the
stream to damming that same stream and
flooding the whole village street, or from
putting snares across the road for the unwary
feet of bemuddled merrymakers, to setting
snares for more unlawful game. Benno
was an adept in this latter accomplishment,
being a pupil of one Wilder, who was
known to all gamekeepers and foresters on
the country-side as a dangerous and incorrigible poacher, although they had never
been lucky enough to catch him in his
nefarious work.

People used to say that Benno's brown

eyes, that always had a mischievous twinkle
lurking in their depths, were exactly like
Wilder's, when Wilder was laughing or
joking with the girls, and they said the
resemblance did not stop there, for Benno
bid fair to become as clever in setting
snares and trapping game as ever Wilder
was. But whether the gossips were right
or not, Wilder was often kinder to the
ragged little vagabond than other people
were, and frequently shared his dinner of
black bread and sausage, while sitting under
a hedge, and more than once bestowed
some odd coins on him, which Benno
promptly exchanged for cakes or confec-
tionery. Once he bought some cigarettes
with the money thus bestowed and proudly
strutted down the village street, with head
held high and smoke issuing in volumes
from his lips, in exact imitation of Wilder,
but it made him so deadly sick afterwards
that, although he boasted to the other boys
of the quantity of tobacco he consumed, no
one ever happened to see him indulging in
cigarettes again.

According to his own accounts, Benno

was a redoubtable hero and hunter. The
stories he told of the battles he had fought
with wild animals that he had encountered
on his mountain expeditions, of the mighty
adventures and hairbreadth escapes he had
experienced, made the other boys wild with
envy; and, seeing this, Benno would invent
still wilder and more impossible adventures.
He had discovered a family of bears, with
whom he was on the most intimate and
friendly terms; he had climbed the topmost
peaks of the highest mountain, and stolen
the eggs from the eagle's nest; he had fought
with and killed the great eagle of which the
hunters spoke with bated breath, or could
only boast of having seen once or twice in
as many years.

"But I," said Benno, "held him by the
neck with one hand and clung to the face of
the rock with the other, while he flapped his
great wings in my face till I thought I must
have fallen into the crevasse, but I held so
fast and kept so tight a hold of his neck that
he could do nothing;—then at last he was
dead."

"Why didn't you fetch him here? The

bürgermeister would have given you ten marks
for him."

"I intended to fetch him—though I would
not have taken ten marks for him, no! nor
twenty either—but in trying to climb down
again I missed hold, and in my efforts to
save myself the eagle fell into the gulch. I
tried to catch it, and nearly fell myself—
I only clutched the feathers, and one came
out in my hand," here Benno stroked the
eagle plume in his old hat with a caressing
touch.

"Is that the feather, Benno?" asked his
hearers, who had listened eagerly to the story,
admiring his bravery and cleverness.

"Yes, that is the feather."

"They say in the village you stole it out of
Anton's hat, when he lay asleep on the hillside."

"Do they? That is Anton's story, I suppose, he didn't like to tell that he gave
his old feather to Rosmarin at the inn for
a seidel of beer, when he had no money left
to buy a drink—but I was there and saw
him."

"Has Rosmarin got it in her hat now?"

"Better ask her," said Benno shortly, and turned the conversation to another topic.

Old Prygel sent his pretty daughter Cari up to the mountain Alm with the cows, and Benno went too to herd them. This sort of work suited Benno; he could lie in the sun all day long, making the mountains ring again with the wild yoddling cries, which no one could make so well as he. The cows and goats learned to obey the shrill sounds and turn their heads and footsteps Almwards, when they heard his call, or follow him obediently when he went singing at the top of his voice to some new slope where the herbage grew more plentifully. Here they would quietly graze while Benno lay on his back staring up into the blue sky, or watching the antics of the chamois as they leaped from crag to crag on the rocks above him, and speculating on their chances of life if he only possessed a gun.

Benno's greatest ambition was to possess a gun, and to be able to kill something. Not that he was of a particularly bloodthirsty disposition—quite the contrary. He had been known to nurse a goat that had got wounded

in a fight, and goats are not the most tractable
of creatures when they are hurt; Benno, however, tended him patiently in spite of the
threatening horns. He had also doctored a
dog with a broken leg. Even an old crow,
whose wing had been broken, received the
most careful attention, which it afterwards
repaid by hopping after the boy, and stealing
his dinner of bread and sausage whenever it
had the chance. They were a disreputable
pair, Benno and the crow; he with his shock
head of curly dark hair, his dirty hands, bare
brown knees and feet, his ragged shirt and
breeches—the crow equally ragged and dirty,
having lost many of its feathers in a fight with
Rattl, the dog belonging to Cari's sweetheart.
Rattl had got the worst of it, but the crow had
come out of the conflict with a bald head and
minus his tail feathers, and, as the lame wing
hung limply to the ground, and trailed as he
hopped about after Benno, he was a very dis-
reputable-looking crow indeed. However, the
damage to his personal appearance did not in
the least lessen his self-esteem, for he picked
as impudently as ever at Benno's bare legs
and toes, if they came too near for his com-

E

fort, and gave a threatening croak if the
dog presumed to eat from the dish till he—
the crow—had satisfied his hunger. Rattl
had grown wise, and, remembering the battle,
he allowed the crow the first innings, and
kept watch for his own opportunity from a
safe distance.

Benno's ambition to kill something was
not therefore due to a want of kindliness
to animals, but rather to a spirit of emula-
tion, and a desire to shine in the eyes of the
village boys as the hero he had always made
himself out to be.

He had seen Fritz coming; in fact, had
watched him with his keen brown eyes for
an hour or more, as the young man toiled
upwards towards the Alm, where his sweetheart was awaiting him. Sometimes he
would be fully in sight, and sometimes lost
to view behind some sheltering slope, again
emerging picking his way lightheartedly.
Benno saw that he carried the new rifle
he had heard so much talk about, and a
wild desire to inspect it more closely seized
him.

Watching Fritz disappear into the Alm,

Benno sauntered after him with an assumed air of careless indifference. He heard the voices of Cari and Fritz within, as he dropped on his hands and knees, and crept silently under the window and along to the doorway. He knew Fritz's custom of setting his rifle and belt in the porch when he entered; he knew also that he would not be permitted to touch the weapon. But in spite of that, Benno crept quietly along close to the wall, unsuspected by the pair of lovers inside, who had so much to say to each other. Yes, there was the rifle, and a beauty it was! Benno's eyes glittered greedily and his hands itched to grasp it; he stretched out his arm and touched it with his finger tips—another little hitch along the ground, and his fingers closed on the stock. Without a sound he drew it from its resting-place, and brought it down beside him, while the pair inside laughed and talked gaily, unconscious of the thief close at hand.

Quickly and noiselessly Benno crawled away and seated himself behind the clump of dwarf pines, with the rifle on his knees and the crow hopping round about him,

evidently as much interested and curious as
Benno himself. Benno examined the weapon
carefully and delightedly. He took out the
cartridges and put them in again with a sigh.
If he only dared to fire it off! He crept out
of sight behind a boulder and made his way
quickly by a roundabout cattle path in the
direction where a little earlier he had seen
a herd of chamois. He could not get near
the spot, but the rifle he knew would carry a
ball several hundreds of feet, and the temptation was too strong. He knew the mountains so well, and was as good a · climber
as the goats he tended, so he scrambled on
out of sight and hearing of the couple at
the Alm. Then he lay down to search
with his sharp eyes for some sign of the
chamois.

Benno's eyes and ears were sharp as
needles, but he was so intent on his watch
for his fourfooted prey that he neither saw
nor heard anything approaching from below
or behind, till he was startled by a voice
close beside him, demanding what he was
doing. It was Wilder. Wilder also carried
a rifle, and any one might have demanded

with reason what he was doing there, but
Benno did not think of that; he only delightedly displayed the beautiful rifle he had
borrowed, and which Wilder's experienced
eye recognised as a masterpiece of its kind.
Wilder took it in his hands, weighed it,
raised it to his shoulder, sighted it as if
taking aim. Benno's quick eye following
the direction, saw a chamois within range.
"Give me the rifle," he whispered; "I want
to shoot it—I will have it," he cried, as he
grasped the man's arm.

"Be quiet, you young fool! I will bring
it down."

"No, no, I will—let go, let go!" and he
seized the stock of the gun with one hand
and the man's arm with the other, struggling
for the possession of the weapon. The man
tried to shake him off, swearing as he did so,
but Benno, seeing the opportunity escaping
him, held on. Loosening the hold of the
man's arm, he seized the barrel of the rifle,
and, giving it a wrench, freed it for an instant
from Wilder's grasp, but in the same moment
there was a blinding flash, a terrible shock,
and Benno felt himself falling—falling—fall-

ing. An agonising pain—then darkness and
silence. The sun sank behind the farthest
peaks, the blue mist rose up and spread itself
over the valley and the lower slopes of the
mountains. The stars came out one by one,
blinking down from the purple sky; then
the moon rose and shed a silvery gleam on
the snowy peaks of the silent mountains,
sending soft beams of tender light caressingly
over snow and grey rock, over fir and shrub,
and on two quiet forms, that lay so still
and white with faces upturned to the starry
heavens; the one on a little plateau, the
other at the bottom of a crevasse some fifty
or more feet below, transfixed on a sharp
needle-like projection of rock.

.　　　.　　　.　　　.　　　.

Down in the village there was a great com-
motion. The men stood in groups round the
smithy, where the blacksmith, hammer in
hand, related the news of the day, while the
oxen brought to be shod stood patiently by,
reflectively chewing the cud, with a kind of
wondering inquiry in their eyes as to the
cause of the unusual delay and excitement.

Teams of horses and mules waited in the

village street, while their drivers stopped to
listen to the news.

Women stood at the doorways discussing
the terrible occurrence that was agitating the
population of the whole valley, while the
boys and girls forgot their lessons and their
play as they listened to the details of the
murder.

Yes! That was the word that was being
passed from mouth to mouth till the whole
village rang with the dreadful sound, and
the very air seemed full of horror.

Poor Wilder had been murdered, and
Fritz, the forester, was to be tried on the
morrow for having murdered him.

Never before had anything so dreadful
happened in the countryside. No wonder
that none of the villagers could think or talk
of anything else. Wilder—the handsome
ne'er-do-well, who had made love to all the
village lassies by turns, who was by far the
best dancer, the best singer, the best shot,
of all the men in the village—was dead, killed
by a murderous bullet, and every one forgot
his faults and failings, forgot that they had
always spoken scornfully of him, forgot that

they had advised their sons and daughters
to avoid him as something dangerous. They
only remembered his handsome face, his
careless good-nature and little helpful ways.
Räsl from the Inn remembered all these and
more, and she wept bitterly for the dead
man, sometimes wept and sometimes prayed
that his murderer might speedily be found and
brought to justice. People said she was like
one crazy with grief, and shook their heads,
wondering why she should grieve more than
other people for the dead man.

At first no one knew whom to suspect of
the dreadful deed, then strange stories began
to be rumoured. Two gentlemen told some
one that they knew Wilder and Fritz the
forester had quarrelled, and that Fritz had
threatened Wilder. So the Burgomaster
and his clerk, and the Notary and his clerk,
sought the two gentlemen and wrote down
all they had to say. When this was done
they sent for Cari and read it to her, and
wrote down all she said. And then the
whole story was written which caused such
dismay in the village. This is what they
were saying to each other.

Fritz the forester went from the village
one morning to see that no traps were laid,
and no snares spread for the game. On his
way he went to the Alm to see his sweetheart, and stayed there while Cari made him
some coffee. While he was there Wilder
came in, and sat laughing and joking. He
asked Cari to give him a kiss, and when she
refused, he said he would take one. Then
Fritz and Wilder had quarrelled. They were
still quarrelling, and Cari was crying, when
two gentlemen, tourists, came in at the door,
and asked for some milk. While they waited
for it and chatted with Cari, Wilder went
away laughing; as he left he made a mocking
bow to the angry Fritz, and said he would
get the kiss sometime when he was not there
to interfere. Then whistling merrily he
disappeared. In a minute or two Fritz went
to the door and saw that his rifle was gone.
He became furiously angry, and rushed out,
saying that Wilder had taken it, and he
would punish him for the theft and for his
rudeness to Cari. Cari called him to come
back, but he would not return.

The two gentlemen, having drunk the milk

Cari brought to them, said "Good-day" to her, then went on their way. They had not left the house many minutes, when they heard the sound of a shot, and one had said to the other, "I hope that fine young forester is not getting himself into some trouble."

They had continued their way, and reached the tourists' shelter, where they met other friends. There they passed the night. At sunrise next morning they continued the ascent of the mountain, and having reached the summit, began to descend again. On the way down they came to a little plateau on the edge of a crevasse, and there lay the dead body of Wilder. Very near to him lay two rifles, one almost a new one, which everybody in the village knew belonged to Fritz the forester.

In vain Fritz denied having seen Wilder after he left the Alm, though he confessed that he had tried to find him, and that being very angry, most likely he would have quarrelled a second time had they met; but he had not seen him, and he went home without his rifle, feeling sure Wilder would return it to him next day.

In vain Cari wept and protested, and in vain the gentlemen urged their opinion that there had not been time for Fritz to reach the plateau when they heard the shot. It was of no use. Poor Fritz was sent to the town to be tried for the murder of Wilder, and everybody knew the case looked very black for him.

No wonder all the village was agog from morning till night, no wonder nothing else could be thought or spoken about. Some said it was clear Fritz had committed the murder in his anger, and others said they could not believe it; Fritz was a fine young fellow, and too good-natured to hurt any one.

There were three women in the village who did not join in the gossip and avoided every one. These three women had wept till the fount of tears was dry, and they could only moan and pray. One of these women was the mother of Fritz the forester; one was Cari, his sweetheart; and the other was Räsl at the Inn—but nobody knew why she wept, for it was not pity for Fritz that brought the streaming tears from her eyes, nor the moans from her lips.

And through all the confusion, consternation, wonder and distress, nobody thought
to ask where Benno was. It was only when
things had quietened down, and people had
time to think of other matters, that one boy
ventured to ask another when he had last
seen Benno. But nobody thought much
about it. Benno had been used to going
and coming at his own sweet will, neither
asking nor waiting for permission. And
Cari was in too much trouble to give a
thought to any one but Fritz. If Räsl at the
Inn thought about him and wondered where
the merry-faced, mischief-loving vagabond
Benno was, she did not say so.

So the time went on, and the day of
Fritz's trial drew nearer and nearer. The
more people thought about the affair the less
hope there seemed that he would ever clear
himself, and even he, sitting in the dreary
prison cell waiting for the day of trial, never
once thought of Benno.

.   .   .   .   .   .

More than an hour's wearisome journey on
the mountains, to the east of the Alm, where

Cari and Benno had spent the long summer days, there is a long narrow opening or defile, caused in days long ago by a split in the mountains. In some places it is scarcely more than a crack, where a man can with difficulty squeeze himself through; in others it is some four or five feet broad, and forms a sort of pathway, that seems to divide the mountain range in two. This pass or defile used at one time to be known and dreaded by travellers as the lurking place of robbers, bandits, and smugglers. Many were the stories told of wicked deeds committed in the dark and gloomy shadows of the mountain pass. At that time gendarmes used to patrol the mountains near the entrance to the crooked narrow path, to protect travellers, who made use of this short cut from the villages on the southern slopes of the great mountain to those on the north. But that was long ago, before the new road was made, a little to the westward, on which horse and mule waggons could travel with safety. Now the narrow pass was seldom or never used. People no longer feared robbers, but they feared the rheumatics and influenza, which lurked in the cold and damp shadows; for even on the brightest summer days the sunbeams seldom penetrated the gloomy recesses of the pass, and in winter it was usually filled to the depth of several feet with snow.

In many places great boulders had fallen from the rocks above, blocking up the pathway, and on those spots where the sun did sometimes shine there had sprung up bushes of the same stunted kind that grew on the mountain slopes, so that, as a road, it was no longer practicable, and travellers, even the most venturesome, avoided rather than sought to explore its dark recesses.

It was said that a lawless gang of smugglers and poachers had their hiding-place and stores in this ravine, but no one had been able to find them, although great rewards had been offered for their capture.

The gendarmes had been through the pass and examined every hole and corner many times, but there was never a sign of a hole likely to hide a smuggler or poacher, let alone his stores, so they had to go back disappointed of the reward they hoped to earn.

But in spite of their failure to find it, such a hiding-place did exist,—and exists still, though now no longer used, because every gendarme knows of its whereabouts.

Some hundred feet from the bottom of the ravine there grew a large clump of dwarf oak trees, that clung to the steep sides of the rock like creeping plants. Hidden behind them was a steep decline, not visible from below, and this decline led through a sort of tunnel formed by a great boulder, having fallen from the heights and wedging itself fast on a ridge. The tunnel thus formed was very low, a man had to crawl for several feet on his hands and knees, then the declivity grew more steep and the roof in consequence was higher, and instead of a narrow tunnel, a good-sized cavern was formed by the fallen boulder. A crack in the rock on one side admitted a little light, though not much, for the crack was partly overgrown with shrubs, still it was light enough to show that this cavern was a sort of store-house, but of a kind that was forbidden by the law. Small kegs containing brandy were piled on one side ; parcels, which might be innocent enough to judge from their appearance, were piled in a corner. Traps, nets, and other adjuncts to the poacher's business lay about, and in another corner hung the bodies of deer and game, ready to be taken to the town and sold.

Nor were these things all the cavern contained. On a bed of moss beside the brandy kegs, and covered with a coarse horse rug, lay the pale emaciated figure of a boy, who gazed anxiously with great dark eyes at two men, who sat conversing in low tones at the end nearest the light. He moved his head and hands restlessly, and moaned a little now and again. The men continued their subdued talk, and after a while the boy dropped into an uneasy sleep. A sound of scraping and shuffling was heard from the tunnel, and the men seemed glad to hear it, for one of them gave a sigh of relief, and a moment later a man made his appearance and was welcomed by the other two.

"How is it with Benno?" asked the new-comer in a low tone.

"Bad," replied the others. "He cannot ast much longer."

" I never knew any one could live so long with a broken back," he added.

" Poor little fellow, it's hard lines for him."

" What news from down yonder ? "

" Bad. In the first place, since we lost Wilder, Karl has been seen too often going with goods, and the gendarmes are under orders to make another search. They may come at any time, and if there comes a snowfall, as it threatens, we shall be tracked. We must clear out of here at once. Down yonder," he continued with a jerk of the head, indicating the village below, " there's an awful upset. Young Fritz is to be tried the day after to-morrow, and they don't think he'll get off. Räsl at the Inn gave me the news ; she's almost broken-hearted ; says she'll never get a quiet hour till poor Wilder's murderer gets his deserts."

" She was always sweet on Wilder, was Räsl."

" Not more than he was on her ; they used to say that that boy "—a little backward movement of the thumb towards the corner finished the sentence, and the other two men nodded comprehendingly.

F

"It's an unlucky business for us as well as for everybody," sighed one of the three. "Wilder was the cleverest among us in getting things disposed of, and now Räsl will not care to help us when he is gone. And there's the boy. What's to be done with him ?"

"Better for him, poor little fellow, if we had left him where we found him. It would have saved him all these weeks of pain and torment. It's a pity, such a jolly little chap as he is."

"We must settle what's to be done about him," said the man who had entered last. "We must clear out of this at once."

"We can't leave the boy."

"We can't take him with us."

"It's hard, very hard for him, but it won't be for long, unless I'm much mistaken."

The men relapsed into silence, each revolving the question within himself.

"Natzi! Martin! Are you there ?"

The weak voice reached the ears of the men, and each started to the side of the sick boy.

There was something of a woman's tenderness in the way in which the one smoothed back the damp curls from the pale brow, and

in the way the other held the rusty tin containing water to the parched lips.

"It won't do to let them hang Fritz, you
know," said the feeble voice. "For one thing,
he hadn't anything to do with it; and another
thing, Wilder is not dead, so there is no sense
in letting Fritz be hanged, is there?"

"Not dead?"

"No! he isn't dead, never has been, he's
been coming now and then to look after me
ever since you fetched me here. I thought
he wanted to keep dark for something, so I
never said a word—but we mustn't let them
hang Fritz."

The men glanced at each other, and the one
stroked the dark curls with his rough hand.

"He was always good to me, was Wilder,"
continued the boy. "He never troubled
about the shot and never blamed me; he
knew it was an accident. But it won't do to
let them hang Fritz! Wilder says he's been
down in the village, trying to explain, but
they take no notice of him nor what he says
—no more than if they didn't see him. He
couldn't understand it, and it worried him,
because he doesn't know what to do."

Martin held the rusty cup to the boy's lips, but he pushed it aside.

"Don't you think you could help *me* to get down to the village? I could tell them, anyway, that Fritz hadn't anything to do with it—then if Wilder comes, they will see there is nothing to make a fuss about. Queer they don't listen to him, isn't it? He does look different somehow; perhaps they don't know him again since he got well."

"What do you think of that?" whispered one of the men as they moved away when the boy dropped into another doze.

"He's going fast," replied the other, "his mind is wandering."

Then glancing at his companion, he said: "Do you think it could be done? He's light enough now, poor little chap. We might manage it with a sort of hurdle slung between us?"

"He can't last much longer, and if he died going down, well it wouldn't make much difference, and there is a chance of him helping Fritz if he lives to tell them, not that Fritz is any friend of ours, but it would please the boy."

They set to work and made a rough litter with branches and moss. On it they gently lifted the sick boy, covering him carefully with the horse-rug that had served for his coverlet.

The sun was setting as the men emerged from the darkness of the cavern with their burden. The change from the perpetual gloom to the brilliant light, that lay like golden sheen over the mountains, made the boy gasp with delight and clasp his wasted hands in ecstacy. The change from the fœtid atmosphere of the hiding-place to the fresh, cool, sunlighted air of the Alps, the glory of the sky, the sound of the breeze, that lifted and played with his hair, the sense of motion, as his bearers swung him carefully between them, was more than the boy could bear, and the great tears welled from under the closed lids, and involuntary sobs shook the wasted form.

The sun sank behind the farthest mountain range, and then commenced the difficult and dangerous descent in the darkness.

Dangerous in the darkness, but for these men it was safer than in the light of day, for they ran less risk of being captured. As it was, they knew they might be seen and fired upon at any moment, but if they were lawbreakers and looked upon as criminals, they were brave enough and tender-hearted enough to risk their liberty for the sake of the sick boy they carried.

It was a terrible journey, two men carrying the litter between them, while the third relieved them in turn or carried the lantern to guide their feet. They stepped carefully, but the road was a rough one, and each jerk or stumble was followed by a moan from the boy, but these grew fainter and fainter and at last ceased.

"He's gone, I think," said one of the men.

"I don't know," replied the other doubtfully; "perhaps he's only fainted, we'd better go on."

So they went on, hour after hour, stopping to rest now and again, but Benno never stirred. Just as the first gleam of the rising sun tinged the topmost peaks of the snowy heights they entered the village at the back of the church,—and paused, looking at each other.

"What shall we do with him?" was the question each mutely asked the other, and they were startled by the reply coming from the lips of Benno himself, whom they thought dead, "Lay me in the church porch, where they found me at first." And the ghost of an amused smile played on the pallid face as the men took up their burden and carried it to the porch, then stood looking sorrowfully down at the poor little figure that tried so valliantly to hide its weakness.

"Now go, Martin. Go now, Natzi, before it gets lighter. Get into the woods as quick as you can, and don't let them catch you. I'll be all right. Some one will soon be stirring, and I'm quite comfortable. You'll be tired! I'm pretty heavy, am I not? But you did splendidly. I'll tell them how good you have been to me. Why! What's the matter? You are not crying, are you! Don't you fret, Wilder and I 'll square up things for Fritz, an' they won't be so hard on you when I tell them how you've looked after me all this time. Good-bye, good-bye. It's good to see the sunshine on the peaks, isn't it? I feel as if I'd get well pretty quick now.

Go now, it's getting lighter. Good-bye, good-bye."

So they left him, and went with quick steps in the direction of the woods. When they reached the corner of the church wall they looked back to see the dark eyes watching them wistfully, but the lips smiled and the wasted hand waved a cheerful farewell.

They were rough crime-stained men, whose liberty and maybe their lives were forfeit to the law; but they felt a choking in their throats, and a dimness in their eyes, as they hurried to reach the shelter of the forest.

A little later, when the sun was spreading its rays over the lower slopes of the mountains, bringing out the brilliant colours of the autumn foliage, when the shutters of the cottage windows were being opened to admit the light of a new day, the door of the vicarage opened, and the priest came out and turned towards the church. He was thinking as he went. When rising from his couch he had remembered that just twelve years ago something had happened.

He had come from his door and made

his way to the morning prayers, as he had
done every day of the thirty years since he
had come to the village to be teacher, friend,
and guide to its people. "Just twelve years
ago!" he was saying to himself. He had
reached the porch of the church and found
there a bundle. In that bundle was an infant,
that had looked up into his face with solemn
brown eyes, and clutched at his hand with its
tiny fingers when he had turned back the coarse
coverlet in which it was rolled. "Just twelve
years ago!" Where was that child? Where
was Benno now? What had become of him
all these weeks? Benno the disreputable,
Benno the incorrigible—the mischief-loving
urchin, the horror of all wise mothers, the
idol of their unwise sons. What had become
of him? An unconscious smile played over
the face of the priest as he recalled in thought
the stories he had heard of the iniquities of
this imp of mischief, this rollicking, boast-
ing, round-faced, curly-haired, dark-eyed
Benno.

The smile broadened as the picture of Benno
in all his mischief rose before his mind's eye,
and it had not faded when he reached the

church porch. He rubbed his eyes—had the twelve years been a dream of the night? Had he only dreamed that the world was twelve years older? But no, the bundle was somewhat larger, and it lay on a bed of moss—and these dark eyes that looked up into his, the fingers that clutched his hand as he turned down the horse-rug? Yes, they were the same, only grown a little larger, the eyes more wistful, the fingers longer, less round and chubby, but they were the eyes and fingers of Benno —Benno the foundling of twelve years ago— Benno the vagabond of to-day.

. . . . . .

Benno lay on a bed, cleaner, whiter, better than he had ever lain upon in his young life before. At one side of the bed sat the priest; on the other knelt Räsl from the Inn, with her face hidden in the bed-clothes. By her side stood an old woman, the mother of Fritz the forester, and near by sat Cari. All three women had wept and prayed over the tragedy of their lives. Now they wept and prayed for the boy, who had told them the story of how that tragedy had come about; but the one who hid her face in the bedclothes wept bitterer tears than the other two, for her trouble was the greatest, because it was locked up in her own heart, and, except the village priest, there were only two who knew of it. One of these was herself, and the other was God.

At the table sat the Burgomaster and his clerk, and the Notary and the schoolmaster, who was the Notary's clerk. They had been writing down the story told by Benno, and when it was finished, the Burgomaster wiped his eyes and tried to read what had been written, but his voice was shaky, and he could not go on. Then the priest took the paper and read it, although his voice was trembling too. But he read on, and the others listened and watched Benno's face the while.

The boy told his story and it was noted word for word just as he gave it :

"You see I wanted to have a look at Fritz's rifle—I never meant to keep it. I took it from the porch and ran away with it. Then Wilder came and took it from me, and· when I tried to get it back to shoot a chamois, the barrel was pointed to Wilder, when it must have gone off and hurt him. I lost my balance and fell I do not know where, but Wilder got better very soon, for he came and talked to me as I lay on the rocks below. He went away for help—he could not carry me himself. He came again and again, telling me to wait and he would bring Räsl and some of the women to help, as the men would not listen to him. At last he came with Martin and Natzi. They and Wilder bore me to a shelter, and all were so good and kind to me. I was pleased to see Wilder looking so well; I had not meant to hurt him. Fritz was never there at all, so you must see that he is not blamed for the accident. Besides, it's nothing to make any bother about. I am getting better, and Wilder is as well as ever he was, so there's no murder. Nobody is dead. Poor Fritz! I am sorry they took him—but it will be all right, and he won't be vexed with me for taking his rifle. It was such a fine one."

"Yes, that's all," he said slowly when the last word had been read. "That's just how it happened, an' nobody's been killed or hurt after all. Martin an' Natzi were very good to me. You won't send the gendarmes after them, will you? And Wilder,—yes, Wilder was always good to me,—he gave me an eagle's feather—I am going to live with Wilder when I'm better. What are you crying for, Räsl? Wilder said,—Ah! here he is.—Now it is all right again.—I've told them all about it, Wilder, an' it's all right now. Is that your hand, Räsl? Just hold mine so, an' I'll go to sleep."

. . . . . .

In the issue, for one of the first days of October 1890, of the *Munchner Nueste Nachrichten*, a paragraph appears which, being translated, reads as follows :—

" On Monday last the inhabitants of Oberau were startled by the news that the innocence of Fritz Kramer the forester, who was about to stand his trial at the present sessions for the murder of a man called Wilder, in August last, had been fully established by the confessions of one Benno, a boy of about thirteen.

"'This boy, who had been missing from the village for several weeks, reappeared in a dying condition, and made a statement to the priest in the presence of the Burgomaster and Notary Public concerning the accident which resulted in the death of Wilder. This statement completely exonerates Fritz Kramer from any complicity in the affair, and he has been released from prison.

"The boy, whose spine had been fractured by a fall, has since died. His statements were clear and lucid, except in one particular; he persisted that Wilder was not dead. This illusion is attributable to the boy's extreme weakness, as it will be remembered that the body of the unfortunate man was discovered on the mountains by some tourists, and was buried two months ago."

Such was the story told in the newspapers. Not much to interest the careless reader, skimming the columns of his morning paper in search of items of political or commercial interest. No, he would glance over the paragraph, and straightway dismiss it from his mind with the possible remark—"Lucky for the forester." But there is much in it of interest to the student of psychology, and of special interest if that same student has a sincere respect and admiration for the simple people of the mountain villages where the tragedy occurred.

I tell the story as I heard it related by those who knew most of the circumstances, and leave the reader to judge for himself whether Wilder is still living, and whether he has been joined by poor little Benno, the vagabond.

THE WARNING SPIRIT

NOT more than three hours' journey by rail from one of the large cities of Europe, lies the valuable estate owned by the Count of K. The present owner is, so far as the direct line goes, the last representative of his name and race—a race for many generations famed for their deeds of prowess and bravery in the wars of their country, as well as, in more remote ages, for the boldness with which they robbed and plundered their neighbours to enrich themselves.

How far this system contributed to the wealth and extent of the estate is not known at the present day, though the descendants of the ancient owners of the soil tell still with bitterness of the wrongs they suffered at the hands of the old lords of K.

Be this as it may; if the estates have thriven and prospered, the owners thereof

have dwindled away, till, when the present
proprietor is laid in the vault, where fifteen
generations of his ancestors have been laid
to rest before him, the race of K. will be
known no more among the living.

It is believed by all the country folk round
about that this event is not far off, for they
say that he has but eighteen months to live,
unless the traditions of his race prove un-
reliable in his particular case ; one of these
traditions being that, from time immemorial,
the lords of K. have received three years'
warning of their death by the appearance of
one of their predecessors ; three years for
repentance, good works, and making their
peace with Heaven.

"Not too long in this case," say the
country people bitterly, for it is hinted that
the page whereon the history of Count K.'s
life is written is not too fair and un-
blemished. Some say that nothing less than
a grave will bury the hatred and loathing
that have grown up in the hearts of his
dependants.

Maybe the stories told of him take colour
from the bitterness still cherished in the

hearts of those who were once masters in the land where they are now servants, for the present tillers of the soil are not the people to forgive or forget injuries, and if they do their duty by their master, it is done with an unsmiling, stolid indifference, that covers in many instances but badly the smouldering dislike they have inherited from their ancestors, for those who have robbed them of their land.

It may be that the stories told by them of Count K. would sound differently if told by some one who loved him; but since his mother, broken-hearted and despairing, lay down her weary head, and sobbed her last breath away in a prayer for the son who had disappointed her, there have been none with sufficient love in their hearts to cast the mantle of charity over the dark record.

A wife's love might have saved him, thought his mother, and she tried to arrange a marriage between him and a bright young girl, daughter to one of their neighbours. But dark stories of the life led by her lover reached the ears of the young lady and her parents, and the engagement was broken off.

This disappointment broke the last band which held the young man in check. He plunged deeper into the mire of dissipation, threw off the slight control his mother had over him, and became an openly avowed materialist and atheist, laughing to scorn the religious observances of his people, and the admonitions of the priests.

In spite of his many extravagances he was singularly penurious, extorting the last farthing from his tenants and creditors, forgiving no part of any debt, and spending as little as possible on anything except his own personal pleasures, or the whim of the moment.

As he grew older, he grew fonder of money for money's own sake. One of his pleasures, after receiving his rents or proceeds from sales, was to count and arrange the gold and notes, which he kept in a safe built into the wall of his own room.

The lock of this safe was a peculiar one, the secret of which was only known to himself. No one but he could open it, even when possessed of the key, though the door closed of itself with a spring.

One day, about two years ago, his valet—who by the way was a new-comer, and had not as yet made himself acquainted with the different members of the family or household—was engaged in arranging his master's wardrobe, when a lady whom he had not seen before entered the room, saying, "Your master needs your help. He is in the safe, go quickly?"

Without stopping to ask a question the man hurried to his master's chamber, where, from muffled sounds and gasping cries from the interior of the safe, he found .that the lady had spoken truly.

The man alarmed the household, and every means was tried in vain to open the door. A locksmith was brought quickly, but his skill availed nothing, and in the meantime the imprisoned count was suffocating.

With more common sense than is usually possessed by his class, the locksmith drilled a couple of holes through the iron door, to admit air, while he proceeded with assistance to file round the lock. This was a work of time, and before it was accomplished the wretched captive was more dead than alive.

Later, when somewhat recovered, the
count called his valet to him, and asked how
it happened that he discovered the accident
of his incarceration. The man explained the
entrance of the lady, and her command that
he should go quickly to his master's assistance.

"What lady? Who was she?" demanded
the count.

"I do not know, I never saw her before,
and I did not stop to think."

"Well for me that you did not," muttered
the count grimly; "but go at once and make
inquiries as to who it was."

The man departed on his errand and
presently returned, puzzled and a little
bewildered. He could find no one among
the household resembling the lady, nor could
he ascertain that any one had any knowledge
of her.

The count seemed disturbed by this
announcement, and after questioning the man
closely as to the appearance of the lady, he
took a pile of photographs and told the man
to look through them, and see if the photograph of the mysterious lady was amongst

them. Glancing at one after another of the pictures, the man picked out one and said, "This is the portrait of the lady, sir!"

The man noticed that his master grew very pale and looked startled, but after a moment's silence he recovered himself with an effort, and said indifferently, "So! that was she! Well, let the matter drop, and see to it that there is no gossiping about the affair. I don't want to be made a laughing-stock for all the clowns in the neighbour-hood. And let there be no talk of the lady." ·

These injunctions, however, came too late. The particulars of the count's narrow escape had already become noised abroad, and it was not long before the story of the visit of the mysterious lady became public property. The servants and retainers of the castle recognised, by the description given by the valet, that she was no other than the late countess—the mother of their master—who had died some ten or twelve years before.

This news startled the young valet con-siderably, the more so as he found the photograph he had so unhesitatingly declared to be that of the lady who had warned him to be that of the late mistress of the castle.

He had some thoughts of leaving his place, but his master, contrary to his usual custom, took a fancy to the young man, probably because he had been instrumental in saving his life, and prevailed upon him to remain. So he stayed on, and his master placed more and more confidence in him, as he grew accustomed to his habits.

About six months after the occurrence narrated, Hans, the valet, was, according to his master's instructions, arranging some letters and papers on his writing table. Becoming for a moment engrossed in a paper he held in his hand, he was startled by hearing a rustling of the letters he had laid to one side behind him. Turning hastily, he saw to his terror and surprise the same mysterious lady who had appeared to him before. Unlike then, he knew now that she was no earthly visitant, and this knowledge almost paralysed him for the moment. Recovering himself, he was about to rush from the room, when, with a commanding gesture, she bade him remain, and listen to a message she would give him for his master.

The man fearfully obeyed, and listened tremblingly to the words that fell in clear, distinct, and awe-inspiring accents from the lips of the lady—listened till his brain reeled and his heart palpitated with fear.

"Tell him these things, nor forget any part of the message I have given you. Furthermore, I charge you that, when you have repeated my words to my son, your master, you will never, while he lives, reveal to living creature what I have this day charged you to deliver to him."

Fixing her eyes on the panic-stricken man, the lady dissolved into thin air, and the valet, with a groan, sank insensible to the floor, where he was afterwards found by his master.

What the message was I know not, nor has the most inquisitive succeeded in eliciting one syllable of its purport from either master or man. But a great and unlooked-for change has taken place. From the life of idle dissipation and wild orgies, that made him hated and feared by all who knew him, the count has become almost a hermit in his castle, secluding himself in his own apartments, denying himself to all his old associates, seeing no one, speaking with no one, except those who have to do with the management of his estates.

The valet too is changed, from the young, careless, light-hearted lad, he has become a serious, thoughtful man, who waits on and attends his master with the kindly solicitude of one who knows that a doom is hanging overhead and must inevitably fall.

There is a mysterious donor who gives largely to charities, and has endowed an asylum for the blind and the deaf and dumb; who, by some unknown means, makes himself acquainted with the needs of the aged and poor and relieves their necessities; pays for the help of some nursing sisters to attend the sick; who has restored the church, repaired the tumble-down cottages, and has led supply of pure water to the villages. The name of this benefactor has not transpired, yet no one questions his individuality. Several children of doubtful parentage, who hitherto have run wild about the cottages, have been sent away to school, and their future provided for. And at the castle itself has appeared a young man, who is the acknowledged heir to much of the vast property; a young man frail and delicate, as if his hold on life was very slight. Though he bears another name, there is too strong a resemblance between his face and the more worn features of the count, to leave room for doubt as to the relationship between them.

The count spends his time in fasting and praying, and one day was found senseless on his knees before the altar, in the little, till now unused, chapel of the castle. The doctor who was called to his assistance was shocked to discover signs of an incurable disease in his patient, and with much reluctance tried to break the unwelcome news that he could not hope to live to become old.

"I know it, doctor; I have known it for more than a year, and I know when it will end. We K.'s have to be thankful that so much time is given us to put our affairs in order. I shall not scandalise the world much longer. The new master will not be a Count of K., but he will be a better man than his— than I have been."

.   .   .   .   .   .

Even while writing the closing words of this story the church bells are tolling at K., and dismay is written on every face, for the news told by the bells is that the young heir and future master lies cold and dead.

The count, looking spectre-like in his wan misery and grief, gives orders that the body shall be placed in the burial-place of his ancestors, and beside the coffin shall be left a place for his own.

For obvious reasons I have not given the name of the Lord of K., though the story as I have given it is known to all the country-side, nor does any one doubt the identity of the mysterious lady—that she is the spirit of the mother of the count, who, true to the traditions of her family, gave her son a timely warning of his fate.

Time will show; and, meanwhile, the priest and others who scout the stories of modern spiritualistic wonders believe un-questionably that God permits such mani-festations as here recorded.

HANS HAUPTMANN'S WARNING

DURING the last twenty-five years I have resided in various parts of Europe, and very many strange stories and unaccountable occurrences have come under my notice. The following narrative of Hans Hauptmann is one of them. It was told to me by himself one morning last year, while I was staying in a German town, near to his native place. He had heard something of the subject of spiritualism in connection with my name, and travelled from his native town, Rattibor, on the Oder, to ask my opinion as to the probable relationship it might bear to many strange facts in his experience. I give the story in his own words, which were translated verbatim.

"You see, fraulein, this is how it was. I am a peasant, and so were my father and grandfather before me. I was never ashamed of being one; indeed, I felt proud of it. I got a farm with my wife. You see, fraulein, my wife was a bit above me. Her father was a landowner, but, though I was only a peasant, I had saved a good bit of money, and Gretchen's father thought, may be, as he had half-a-dozen daughters, it would not be a bad plan to get one off his hands to a well-to-do peasant. So he and my father arranged it between them; that's the way such things are managed in Germany. I liked Gretchen well enough, and we got on very well, but, as I said, she was a bit above me, and had got notions that I could not take with. She didn't like farm and dairy work, but I was master, and she had no choice but to work. I had been brought up to work hard all my life and hated to see any one about me with idle hands. Well, Gretchen got weakly and delicate and couldn't go about after the women, or superintend the dairy-work, and it made me mad to see the waste. You know, fraulein, what servants are when the mistress's eyes are not on them.

"Well, in a few years we had four children—two boys and two girls. As soon as

they could toddle they had to go to work.
I was determined to bring them up to it
from their cradle, for I couldn't tolerate
Gretchen's fine lady-ways, and I determined
that my children should be either farmers or
farmer's wives.

"I was growing quite rich.   I had the
finest farm in the province and the finest
cattle, and I might have ranked with the
landowners, but I didn't want to do that.
I had little or no education, and I had no
wish to push myself into company where I
would have to take a low seat.   As a peasant
I stood at the head of my class, and held
a dignity of my own among them that I
would have lost had I tried to rank as one
of the landowners.

"Gretchen wanted to educate the children, and send the boys to college; but I
soon put a stop to that nonsense, and she
knew better than to say much more on that
matter; but she went about the house so
pale and dispirited, that her very looks were
a reproach to me, and I grew to hate her for
it.   She never reproached me in words, but
her looks were sufficient.

"What did it matter to her whether we were rich or poor? A fine talk it would have been for the town if Hans Hauptmann's sons were sent to college; no, they should be farmers as their grandsires had been.

"No, fraulein, you are right, it was not kind of me. I know now, when it is too late. I was a brute to Gretchen and the children, and how bitterly I have repented you shall know.

"The eldest boy was about seventeen, and the next to him was Elia; she would be about sixteen. Gretchen had given them a bit of education, besides what they got at the village school, and they were wonderfully quick children, not like the two younger ones. Both of them came to me one day, when I had made a good sale and was in a good humour, and began pleading to be sent to Leipzig to school. The boy wanted to study medicine. Well, fraulein, I felt so enraged that, Heaven forgive me, I lifted my hand and struck at the girl. She staggered and fell. The boy Fritz, with his face crimson with passion, raised his hand against me, but it was to his own sorrow, for rage made me incapable of remembering that it was a lad, slender as a girl, that I was dealing with. I beat him without mercy and left them.

"I entered the house, and the sight of Gretchen's face brought into my mind that it was also her wish to send the children to school, and I fancied she had sent them to me. My rage burst out afresh at the thought, and I hurled a heavy drinking-pot at her, felling her to the ground; and then I went to bed. You are shocked, fraulein, and I don't wonder at it. Yes, I was a wretch.

"As well as being a farmer, I used to do something in the weaving; and though I was tolerably rich, I thought a little more of this world's goods would do no harm, so I determined to take up this business more thoroughly and try my luck.

"I had a large outbuilding fitted up with looms, obtained the necessary materials, and arranged all ready for commencing the work. I had engaged some women, and rejoiced at having now found means to occupy Gretchen's attention, and find her plenty to do, without talking of sending the children to college.

"Everything was ready for work. It was late in the evening, and, chuckling to myself at the thought of the profit that would accrue to me from this new branch of labour, I locked the door, made all secure, and went off to bed, putting the key of the room under my pillow. You must understand, fraulein, I had had a new lock put on that door—one of those patent locks which no key but the right one could open.

"Next morning, bright and early, came the women to work, and I went to the place to see them commence, but, to my rage and astonishment, I found every thread on each of the twelve looms cut — a week's work wasted by some malicious person. Vexing? Yes, it was vexing, and, God forgive me, I vented my rage on Gretchen and the children.

"In another week the looms were in readiness. Again I made all fast, but this time I locked Gretchen and the children in their rooms, for I suspected them, in spite of their protestations. Again the women came to work, and a second time the threads were found to be cut. What was I to think? I

H

went mad. I knew my wife and children had nothing to do with it this time, but I dared not vent my rage on any one else, so they had to suffer.

"A third time I tried the looms, and a third time with the same result.

"I used to drink sometimes, and now I drank deep enough—deeper than ever. I turned Gretchen and the children out of the house, and they went to a neighbour's for shelter.

"I drank and drank until, in stooping to unfasten my boots, I reeled and fell to the ground. Though my brain seemed clear enough, my limbs failed me, and I was incapable of rising. While lying on the ground, like a beast, I saw an old man beside me. I growled out an inquiry as to his business— coming into a man's house uninvited. I tried to kick him, but my feet refused to do my will. The man's face seemed to be familiar to me, but for some time I could not remember where I had seen him. At last it jumped into my mind—it was Gretchen's father; but then at the same moment I remembered he had been dead ten years. That recollection paralysed me, and I could only lie still and stare at the old man. At length he said, 'Take care, Hans Hauptmann; take care! I have watched you for a long while. You are driving my Gretchen to her grave by your miserable greed. Take care how you treat her and her children, or woe be to you!'

"Well, fraulein, how I passed that night I cannot tell, but next day I cursed myself and the spirits I had imbibed, and attributed the old man's visit to the effects of the drink.

"Gretchen and the children came home, and without any provocation on their part I ill-used them. The boy, Fritz, tried to take his mother's part against me, but, infuriated, I put him and Elia to the door and bade them never enter it again. You may well be shocked, fraulein, yet it is all true—every word; to my own shame I say it. After this my cattle sickened and died, two or three in a day sometimes; a plague seemed to have broken out among them. I tried to sell them, but no one would buy, and so they died.

"One night—this time I was not drunk—that old man came again. This time I raved at him—swore at him—and told him it was he who had brought all these disasters upon me, and if they were not stopped, I would murder his daughter and the children to spite him; but he only said, 'Take care! Hans Hauptmann! A second time I warn you—take care!' I would not take this warning, and my losses only made me worse.

"Again the old man came. This time it was after I had beaten Gretchen until she lay insensible. Then, and only then, did my mad passion cool. I received the old man's warning, as before, with oaths and curses, but, woe is me! two days later all my cattle, of which I had been so proud, were dead, and I retired to rest no better for the knowledge. My wife and children had grown to fear my step and hated my presence in the house. It was only two nights since the old man's last warning. I had scoffed and sworn at him, and now I lay dreaming of his features. I must have been in a deep sleep; I was aroused by some one pulling me from my

bed and throwing water upon me. It was
Gretchen. Stupid and half-blind I staggered
from my bed, demanding what was the matter.
'Come! come! the house is on fire! For
the good God's sake save yourself!' cried
Gretchen. I did save myself. Gretchen
also was saved, but my two younger children
—my poor girl and boy—they were gone—
burned—dead! 'Why did you not let me
burn?' I asked of Gretchen, when I remembered how she must have crossed the burning
floor to reach me. 'You are my husband and
my children's father,' she answered with a
sob; 'I could do no less.'

"I had been rich before, but now I had
nothing—nothing but the bare land. My
well-filled barns were destroyed — my cattle
dead—my house and my two poor children
burned. Surely no man on earth was so poor
as I, nor any who had such a terrible burden
to bear. How I made my peace with Gretchen
I can not tell; I know I felt I was too low for
forgiveness; but she is an angel, fraulein, if
ever there was one on this earth. She for-
gave me, and she loved me in spite of all,
and it is to her kindness and help I owe all

the good which has come to me since that terrible time.

"Fritz and Elia came back to us. I worked hard for them night and day, and now Fritz is a doctor in Münich, and is called a clever and a learned man, whose kindness goes a long way toward curing his patients. And Elia, my dear Elia, she writes books—such stories that, when I read them and know that they all came out of her pretty head, I think to myself, 'That's the girl I put out on the road that bitter winter's night.' But she has forgiven me all that, though I have not forgiven myself.

"Now, you see, fraulein, I heard the doctor talk of spiritualism and the strange things the spirits do, and I thought maybe you would be able to tell me if it really was Gretchen's father that came to me, or whether it was my imagination. It could not be my imagination; I never imagined anything like that in my life before; indeed, never anything, unless it were some new machine or other to do more work; but even in that my imagination would not hold out.

"I do not know what I should have been

by this time, for I was nigh mad with love of
money in those days. It's near upon fifteen
years since then, and I am getting to be an
old man now. And Gretchen, my wife, is very
dear to me. When I think of all the mis-
spent years I have lived, and the terrible life
I led her, I feel very loth to believe that the
old man was only an image I had conjured
up, because, you see, fraulein, if it were the
old man, I can hope that I, too, may live in
another world and see my poor children again,
and beg their pardon, and make some amends
to them and Gretchen for the misery I inflicted
upon them."

PEPI

TOLD BY A CLAIRVOYANTE

HE was leaning on the fence, smoking a cigarette, and looking at us as we seated ourselves in the carriage. He nodded, smiled, and exchanged a merry word with Natzi, our coachman, wished us a pleasant journey, and then, just as we drove from the door, he came and tucked in the rug about my feet more securely, lifted his hand to his brow with a military gesture, and smiled again as I thanked him.

"Who is that handsome fellow?" I asked, when out of hearing.

"That is Pepi."

"Oh! Is that Pepi?" I looked back at the handsome figure leaning carelessly against the gate post, blowing little rings of smoke away over his head, for the amusement of the maids who watched him admiringly.

The sound of their light laughter reached us till we drove round the corner, and the group was hidden from our eyes and ears.

Pepi was a soldier, had been a soldier a year and a half, and now at Whitsuntide had leave of absence for three whole days.

No wonder there were extra rejoicings in the village. It was something to have Pepi home. The fun was no fun at all when he was not there to lead it.

There wasn't a chamois hunter who could boast of his prowess as Pepi could. Why, when he was only eighteen, he had brought back from the Zugspitz three of the finest animals that other hunters had been following for days.

As for Edelweiss, nobody knew so well where it grew as Pepi did, and, even if they had known, there were none so daring as he, or would risk so much to pluck it. Where a chamois could obtain foothold, there was foothold also for Pepi. No one knew t' e mountains as Pepi knew them; no one's eyes so keen or feet so sure; no yodel so prolonged or musical. He would trudge off even when a little lad with his

flock of goats to pasture on the green slopes,
and then he would yodel away till the mountains echoed again, and visitors to the Alpine
villages would stroll out to listen to the
music, rendered so sweet and strange by the
echoing repetition in the clear sparkling air.

As for dancing, there was not a lad in a
dozen villages who could dance the Schuhplattl as Pepi could. When the sound of
his wooden sabots was heard on the floor,
and the shrill cry, and clapping of hands on
the thighs began, then girls and boys, men
and women, old and young, rushed . to see,
to applaud, and admire, and finally to join
in the strange wild dance, leaping, twirling,
clapping of hands, of thighs, of shoes, strange
cries, crouching, stooping, twisting, turning,
then a leap, a stamping of feet, a bird-like
cry, and amid shouts of laughter and panting
ejaculations of his partners, Pepi would stop
and empty his stoup of beer in a draught.

It was not remarkable that he was greatly
in request, careless, reckless, merry, good-
natured Pepi; the life and soul of all the
merry - making, the expeditions, and the
sports of the young people.

No wonder that Anna Marie, at Whitsuntide, fixed her wedding day so that the feast should be graced with Pepi's handsome face and rich fun. The girls put on their gayest neckerchiefs, and polished up the silver ornaments on their belts and necklaces, and brought out the chains and brooches which had lain by for years.

They were up bright and early to seek the Alp roses to fasten in their gold-trimmed soft felt hats. It was not often nowadays they had the chance of such fun and merriment, for Pepi had been a soldier now a year and more, and there were none like him.

No wonder the girls practised the steps of the Schuhplattl so that they might have a chance of dancing with Pepi at the wedding feast, for Pepi was very particular that his partner should not shame him in the dance, and since he had been away in München, he had grown quite fastidious about his partners' proficiency and grace.

The Whitsuntide of 1894 had been fuller of enjoyment than most holidays.

First, there had been the grand church festival and procession. Pepi had himself

carried the holy crucifix from the church
in the village to the church on the hill,
chanting the litany as he went, followed by
all the boys, girls, young men and maidens,
men and women, old and young; up through
the long street, out to the open country, up
the steep hill, past the twelve stations of
the passage of our Lord, where they rested
the crucifix at each one as they passed. The
people prayed aloud as they went. Then
they entered the church where the priest
received the holy emblem from his hands,
and blessed the kneeling people. .

Then they carried it back to its place in the
church, and Pepi and the crowd dispersed.

Then came Anna Marie's wedding, and
Pepi had been the one to waken the bride at
four o'clock in the morning with a serenade.
Then he and his friends had gone to the
bridegroom's house, and roused him from his
slumbers.

It was Pepi who headed the procession to
bring the bride and bridegroom through the
village to the church, where the kindly old
priest was awaiting them, and who, the
ceremony over, led them to the different

inns where the people were assembled to congratulate them.

Later it was Pepi who summoned the guests to eat, and drink, and dance at the feast prepared for the happy pair.

It was Pepi who stole the bride and hid her away, where none of the wedding guests could find her, and when at last tired of seeking, the bridegroom offered a ransom for her recovery. It was Pepi who received the payment which was used to supply the merry-makers with the cakes and ale of the village.

Then on the next day when they "played theatre," it was Pepi who was the life and soul of the whole performance.

Now the last day of the holidays was come, and the villagers had settled down to their work in the fields, the tending of their flocks of goats and sheep, or the pasturing of the herds of pretty cream and dun cows on the mountain slopes.

Many had already been sent up to the Alms in the mountains for the summer, and as we drove slowly round the foot of the snow-crowned monarchs of the Alpine heights, we met little groups of lads and lasses re-

turning from the Alms, where they had spent
their holidays in visiting the pretty "Sen-
nerinen" in their mountain homes. Lonely
enough were the inhabitants of these Alms.
There was the solitude of the eternal hills,
and the silence of the mountain fastnesses,
broken only by the tinkling of the cowbells,
or the rushing of the torrents as they made
their way from the snowy peaks that seemed
to pierce the blue of heaven, down to the
green valley that lay like a jewel at their
feet.

The holidays were over and the everyday
duties must be taken up; with light hearts
or heavy hearts the work must be resumed.

The afternoon had been gloriously fine,
and our drive had extended itself beyond our
first intention. It was three hours later when
we returned to the village, and caught the
sound of the tolling of the church bell.

Who can it be, Natzi? Who can be dead?
we ask.

"It is old Bartl, I expect," replied Natzi,
"he was dying this morning. The priest
carried the holy sacrament to him. He is
old and has been long ill. God rest his

soul!" and Natzi crossed himself devoutly as he uttered the prayer.

Driving in through the gateway I saw Pepi standing in almost the same spot as when we set off. I noticed him carelessly, and a comical idea crossed my mind that he had been standing there during the three hours of our absence.

He did not come to our assistance as when we left, but that was nothing wonderful. These mountaineers are seldom inclined to do the work of a lackey.

As we passed him he looked up and our eyes met. It was Pepi. There could be no mistake about that. But such a Pepi! God forbid that my eyes may ever again see the face of one of His creatures so distorted with anguish, misery, and helplessness, as were the features that raised themselves to mine.

My heart seemed for an instant to stand still. I leaned forward, his eyes still on my face.

"Look!" I said, grasping the hand of my companion, "what is it with Pepi?"

At the same instant our host, the hôtelier,

came to assist in our descent from the carriage.

"What is it with Pepi?" said my friend, repeating my question inquiringly. She had not noticed him with her short-sighted eyes, and wondered at my remark.

Again I eagerly asked, "What is the matter with Pepi?"

"Ah! Gracious lady, such a terrible thing has happened since you left; a calamity so dreadful! Pepi is dead!"

"Pepi dead? Why, Pepi is here," I interrupted, glancing round to where he stood, but he was gone. I went to the gate and looked round the corner, but there was no one in sight.

The little group on the veranda stood discussing something, and Natzi was listening with horror-stricken features as he stood by his horse's head.

"Yes," our host was saying, "Pepi is dead."

He went from the gate when we had driven away, he had joined some companions, and they together had gone through the village and up one of the mountain paths, towards a deep gully spanned by a bridge over a waterfall. It is a favourite place of resort on hot summer days, the high cliffs on either side keeping out the sun; and the spray of the leaping, tumbling waters, keep the grasses, mosses, and trees of a cool refreshing verdure.

It is not without its dangers, for the narrow footpath winds zigzag up the face of the damp slippery rock, and the bridge which spans the torrent is at a great height, and looks a frail enough foothold, its slender framework of iron looking almost like the work of some clever spider.

Up this slippery footpath had Pepi climbed, followed by his companions. On reaching the bridge, he was the first to cross. Pausing in the middle he shouted to them not to follow. " Boys," he said, "*I have overstayed my leave, and I dare not go back.*" Then he flung himself backwards over the slender rails and disappeared.

Horror-stricken they had rushed down the steep pathway, and there at the foot, crushed among the boulders over which the water was foaming and dashing, lay the crushed,

I

mangled body of handsome, merry, light-hearted Pepi.

Sadly enough they bore him back to the village, but who was to take the news to the poor old father and mother? Who could comfort them?

Pepi had overstayed his leave. He had done it twice before and had been punished. Yet again had the temptation of fun and merry-making been too much for the light-hearted, careless boy, and on awakening to the consciousness that he had again offended against the military laws, and overstayed his leave, he dared not face the punishment and degradation he knew awaited him. He preferred rushing headlong into the Unknown, forgetting all the teachings and lessons of life; forgetting the exhortations of the priest who had confirmed him, and heard his first confession; forgetting the mother who bore him, loved him, waited for him with anxious heart, urging him to remember his duty; forgetting the father who was so proud of his handsome son's prowess and cleverness; forgetting everything but the fact that he had infringed the law and must be punished.

And this his proud untamed spirit could not brook. So he took his fate in his own hands, and rushed uncalled for, unprepared, and ignorant, into the other world.

All this I heard repeated over and over again, yet my thoughts circled round and round one fact, and I could not get away from it—*Pepi was not dead, for I had seen him.*

All night long the pale anguished features, and helpless bewildered look in the dark eyes, haunted my couch, and I rose early, unable to sleep.

Descending to the garden, I glanced almost in fear towards the spot where I had seen him last. He was not there, and I began to wonder if the scene had not been after all a part of a dream, conjured up in the night, by the thoughts of the tragedy which had been enacted during the previous afternoon.

Soon came news which almost paralysed the village, and set the people gazing fearfully at one another, not believing their ears. The priest had refused to bury Pepi. All that morning it seemed as if some awful calamity had fallen over the whole village.

Everywhere a dull silence reigned. If people spoke it was in hushed whispers. Men neglected their work and sat or stood in silent groups at corners. Women moved noiselessly and tearfully about their household tasks, scarcely daring to look in each other's faces. The church door stood open. Men and women went in and out, and some knelt to pray, while others wandered aimlessly about, or sat on the church steps, their faces bent moodily downwards, and the rosary between their roughened fingers.

Only in one cottage was the sound of wailing that would not be stilled, only one voice that would not be silenced, one heart that would not cease to pray for mercy for the soul of the boy she had borne.

Was it not enough to lose the bright happy life that had gladdened the home and hearts, for nearly twenty-three years! But that his soul, the immortal soul, that God had given into his keeping, should be lost for ever, consigned to eternal perdition, to everlasting torment. No! no! she would not be quiet; she could bear to lose her boy, but this she could not bear.

"Gracious Lady! help me, help me."

Sore at heart, with pity for the grief we could not assuage, we left the stricken mother and returned to our home. The tears blinded me as I thought of the agony I had witnessed, and I longed to do something to help, but I was a stranger in a strange land, and an alien in faith and religion. I could do nothing.

I put out my hand to open the gate, and there before me, pale, horror-stricken, agonised, and pleading, was the face of Pepi —Pepi as I had seen him the day before in the same place. But so changed, with a change awful and indescribable. It was only a moment of time, yet in that moment I understood the terror in his face, and knew that he, though no longer in the body, was suffering the torments of hell. He had begun dimly to understand that he had not only disobeyed the command of his superior officer, but in escaping the consequences of his folly, he had broken the law of the Church, and he was afraid of the condemnation of the priest—afraid of everlasting damnation.

Poor, misguided, ignorant soul.

I sprang panting up to my room, and sat down to think. Then I made my way to my friend, and said, " I cannot bear this—let us go to the priest."

So we went.

Poor old man, his trouble was scarcely less than that of the stricken parents, for his was the hand that must deal the crushing blow, and his heart was sore.

"We are strangers, sir," we said; "strangers to your land and your faith, yet the trouble of your flock lays heavy on us also. Can nothing be done to lighten the terrible burden that has fallen on them? Must this thing be?"

"My daughter, the Church, says if any man lay violent hands on himself, being of sane mind and whole, the same offends against God, and may not hope for the blessing of the Church. Think, if I pass this by lightly, how many of my flock, reckless, careless as he, may follow his terrible example. It is very hard, my daughter. Pepi was my favourite among all the village youth. Yet what can I do? He has offended against the laws of God and the Church."

"But, sir, God has said, 'Vengeance is Mine, I will repay.' Pepi is beyond the reach of the Church; he is in the hands of God. Do not be harder than He; do not punish the wretched parents, who have done nothing wrong, and who are bowed down with misery. Pepi must suffer for his folly, but let not the punishment fall on the innocent."

It was no difficult matter to plead with the kindly old priest. It was easy to see that the struggle between kindliness and fancied duty was an unequal one, and when we left him, he had promised to "take the question to God and the Saints," and ask them for guidance.

All that evening we waited anxiously for news. The same silence weighed over the village, and the same gloomy faces met us at every turn. Evening drew on, and the prayer bell summoned the people to vespers, and they gathered together silently in the church.

The service began, and then, as the old priest lifted up his voice in a prayer for the soul of the dead, it was as if an angel had lifted the burden from their hearts, and the silence was broken. Tears indeed streamed from the eyes of the people, but the gloom was gone. Pepi's soul was saved!

Next morning they buried him. The reaction from the gloomy broodings to the hope of salvation was almost too much, and to me who, watching from my window the funeral procession pass by, headed by the priest with bell, book, and candle, and all the praying chanting crowd following, it seemed almost jubilant.

I was glad indeed that the priest had decided to bury the dead Pepi in the consecrated ground with all the ceremonies of the Church; glad for the sake of the miserable parents who had lost their boy; glad for the whole village, for indeed if Pepi's sin had been so great, then there were none of his companions much less guilty, inasmuch as they had tempted him to his folly during the past few days.

I was glad for the dead Pepi that he should rest in peace in God's acre. But the living Pepi, what of him? What does he think now of his sin? I would give much to know, yet as I pass the gate where I saw him standing those two dreadful days, I turn my face away, for the memory of that agonised face and pleading eyes rises up again, and I dread to encounter them once more.

Sometimes I wonder if it was any satisfac- to him that the Church refrained from con- demning him; if the knowledge of the first decision of the old priest had increased his misery, when he found that, in endeavouring to escape the penalties of his fault, he had only made his punishment greater.

.   .   .   .   .

Looking down from the verandah this afternoon (*Whitsuntide* 1896), looking at the blossoms on the chestnut tree just opening their rose and white pyramids to the sky, a hand parted the branches, and a face peered up at me from behind the leafy screen. It was Pepi. Not the palid drawn features of Pepi as I had seen him the two last times. Nor yet the laughing, handsome, merry-faced Pepi, that arranged the rug about my feet that fateful Whitsuntide, now two years agone, —but still it was Pepi.

The despair and agony were gone from his face. Calm and sorrowful it was still, but in- stead of the pleading terror in the dark eyes, now gleamed a steadfast earnest purpose. No longer the merry, light-hearted, reckless dancer on life's highway, but one who has learned that he has thrown away God's greatest gift, the gift of life, and yet must live on, and suffer for his folly.

I am glad I have seen him once more, and seen him as I saw him, for now I can put away the memory of the terror-stricken features, and remember the calm, serious, earnest look of the face which gazed at me from the branches of the flowering chestnut tree; and can think, "Perhaps at last all will be well."

THE MILL STREAM

THERE stands a house by the side of a stream
—the Mill Stream they call it, for, a little bit
higher, like a ghost in its garment of flour,
stands the Mill, and through it comes rushing
the stream with a whirring, a churring, and a
clang, making the wheels and machinery turn
and writhe, and the stones to revolve till the
head is dizzy, and ears are deaf with the noise
and the clatter.

The men, like phantoms in grave-clothes,
are holding high revel, laughing and talking;
jumping about in a manner not seemly to
spirits of men from the churchyard. They
work and whistle and sing, receive the corn
from the farmers, grind it to meal in the mill,
and deliver the same to its owners.

The stream, after doing its duty in turning
the wheel for the miller, goes roaring and
foaming and dashing, twisting and turning

and clashing, twirling and curling and eddying round, as though in vexation of spirit;
splashing and crashing and rushing along
with a din and a roar and a noise, like an ill-
humoured giant disturbed in his sleep, or the
distant verberation of thunder.

Lower still the tumult is over, the roaring
and clashing have ceased, and the stream
moves placidly on between the hills, as though
nothing could ruffle its smoothness, reflecting
the trees and bushes which grow on its
borders, smiling up in the face of the heavens,
reflecting its light or its darkness, the sunlight, the moon, and the starlight, with an air
serene and happy, like one who has passed
through the troubles of life, experienced all
of life's evils—and having overcome them, is
now content not to heed them.

In the house by the stream dwelt the
miller,—the miller, his wife and his daughter.
Six days of the seven he worked in his mill,
from early to late in the summer, from dawn-
ing till dark in the winter. Stout, brawny,
and strong was his frame; in years perhaps
numbering fifty—though of this no one could
be certain; for the hair on his head and his

face was as white as the hair of a man full of years, the term of his earth-life completed; white with years, said some; and some, with the flour of his neighbours.

When the day's work was over and evening had come, he would sit with a neighbour and gossip of crops, of cattle, of markets, of this thing and that, till the hour drew nigh for retiring; then the doors are closed, the curtains drawn, and the pipe replaced in his pocket; composing his features, the round face growing lengthy and long as becomes the solemn occasion, he draws his chair to the table, inclining his head to his wife without speaking, whereupon she, understanding, inclines also her head to her daughter. Then taking their seats they sit silent, with eyes downcast and fingers demurely folded. With reverend looks and sober mien he opens the well-thumbed volume, and takes from between its leaves the spectacles placed there to mark the pages last read.

These fixed on his nose, and the lesson picked out for the evening, the head of the house commences expounding the Scriptures.

He reads of the children of Israel in Egypt, of the trials they suffered in bondage; how the Lord sent a man of their race to the king, to beseech him on behalf of the people, to lighten their labours, and let them depart in peace to the land of their fathers; how the king, much persuaded and counselled, consented at last to grant the prayer of the captives; how the Lord, then, did harden the heart of the king, and made him repent his decision; how the Lord in anger sent plagues and disorders and darkness and death: first softened the heart of the king by affliction, and then, for some righteous reason, did harden again, and cause him to recant the promises made in his weakness; and then, to punish the king's hardness of heart, and to publish His own just indignation, the Lord did send down an angel from heaven to kill all the first-born of Egypt.

In tones solemn and slow the miller read, pausing now and again with uplifted eyes, that glanced through the horn rim of his glasses, to mark the effect of his words on his hearers; and when he had finished the chapter he closed with this observation—

"Such are the wonderful ways of the Lord, and His mercy endureth for ever."

"Methinks," said Ruth, the miller's young daughter, "that the mercy in this case was a-wanting; it scarcely was just to punish the nation because the king had incurred His displeasure; and when He Himself hardened the heart of the king, was it right He should punish the people?"

The miller looked up in angry displeasure. "Things," he said, "are coming on strangely, if this be the way children talk to their elders. Who taught you to judge of the Lord or His mercy? Not your mother, I ween, nor would the parson give you such ill-advised counsel. Surely the Lord may do what He likes with His own, without asking permission of those He created. Flee to your closet, and pray that His wrath may not overtake you for daring to question His justice."

It chanced at that time that the wife of the miller was engrossed with the cares of her household, her larder and dairy, and all the things thereto pertaining. As soon as her husband had gone to the mill she would be

up and a-stirring; a-smoking and drying of
bacon and ham, a-pressing and moulding of
cheese, stirring and scolding and bustling
around, taking care that no fingers were idle.
Such scrubbing and scouring, and brightening
of pans, such washing and rubbing of dishes,
preserving of fruits and baking of bread,
pies, pastry, and delicate dishes.

For a stranger was coming that day to
sojourn in the house of the miller; a slender
young stripling of twenty-five summers was
about to seek, in the house of the miller, the
good health he had lost in the city; "lost
for the want of good food," said the wife of
the miller; so she laid a fresh stock in her
larder, determined no efforts of hers should
be spared to recruit the weak health of the
stranger. Then when he arrived, pale, weary,
and weak, she gave strict instructions to her
daughter to tend well the wants of her
guest, that he might not grow weary and pine
for his home in the city. And also she gave
her grave counsel to hold in subjection her
childish and hoydenish spirit; to be prudent
and grave, and hold herself with all maiden
decorum; to neglect not her spinning nor

weaving, lest the stranger should take back
a tale to the town of the unthrifty child of
the miller. Still further she gravely advised
her to study her Bible and psalm-book, to
impress on her mind the words of the Lord,
and pray for His grace to redeem her; to
have faith in His wisdom and mercy; not to
think and make seditious speeches like the
sons and daughters of Belial, for they suffer
severely, for all their rebellion and treason,
who question the right of the Lord.

Thus with motherly counsel did she talk
to her daughter, but alas! the maiden was
fair, and Philip, the stranger, was comely.
Moreover the stranger was sick. Right well
the girl observed her mother's behest, and
looked well to the wants of the stranger.
She would sit by his side on the bank while
he fished in the river, or, when he was weary,
would sing with soft musical cadence the
words of the Psalmist; or sometimes he'd
sit by her side at the wheel and help her to
feed it; but somehow, their fingers entangled
the thread, the wheel would buzz round, the
thread snap and snarl, and Ruth would look
up demurely—"It did it itself, I assure you

K

—I really cannot understand it." The good wife, perplexed, would disentangle the thread and sigh for her daughter's shortcomings, and think of the time when she herself was a girl and worked by the side of her mother —had worked and sung psalms; would think of the flax and the wool she had carded and spun, of the piles of fine linen her own hands had woven, ere becoming the wife of the miller. It was sad to think how far maidens had fallen short since then.

Philip was grave for his years, with much thought and much learning. He talked to the maiden, and she loved to listen of the why and the wherefore of things, the reason for this and for that. And things that had once been to her a puzzle were explained and made clear to her mind. He would talk of the Scriptures, of the monk who translated them from the scripts and quaintly writ letters on parchments; would discourse of the lives of the holy apostles, their fastings, their trials and teachings, extolling the greatness and goodness of God who inspired them and gave them such courage.

And the maiden would listen intently with

wondering eyes, admiring deeply the knowledge possessed by her teacher. When Philip
encountered her soft gaze he grew greatly
perplexed and bewildered; and found his
heart palpitating, in a manner both wild and
unseemly. Then to his delight and amaze-
ment he discovered, that while he had been
teaching he too had been learning a lesson,
and, not to seem selfish or greedy, he taught
it again. This was the lesson of love, which
she to the full comprehended. And thus
months passed away, and still at the house of
the miller the stripling yet lingered, though
his face had grown ruddy, and his limbs stout
and strong, with good health. He "could
study much better with Ruth by his side,"
was the excuse he made to the miller. And
the miller, well pleased that his child should
have won the heart of Philip the scholar, was
content to see the bright faces of the twain,
as they walked hand in hand through the
meadows, or talked of the time when the two
should be one, and live in a cottage together;
how Philip would teach the good tidings to
men, and point out the straight road to
heaven; how Ruth should help in the care

of his flock, and teach in the school of a
Sabbath; how, like two happy children, they
ever would be a-living and loving each other,
for, till death should divide them they never
would part; and perhaps they might both die
together, like those who had lived undivided
on earth, and death did not try to dissever.

At length the autumn had come, and
Philip must go to the city—must go to the
city, and there be ordained by the bishop.
Then after a while he'd return to the mill,
to claim his young bride from her father.
The day of departure too quickly drew near,
and Ruth, with her face pale and tearful,
clung tight to her lover, a-trembling with
fear.

"Suppose you fell sick," she said, "as you
did once before in the city; suppose you
should die and I never to see you! Something clutches my heart, and I seem like to
die with the feeling; and in spite of all
reason there's something that tells me, that
when you depart in the morning I never
again shall behold you. Something will
happen, one of us will die, and we shall meet
no more till we wake up in heaven." It was

in vain that he soothed her, for, strange to
say, he too felt the same premonition, but
laughing, he said: "If I die I'll come to
you; for I love you too dearly to leave you;
even heaven itself would be dreary and dull,
if you were not there beside me."

Thoughtless he spoke to beguile her strange
fears, but she, in her terror, believing, repeated his words with so solemn an air, that
their import did startle him strangely. Then
holding her close to his heart, as he spoke
in tones that were solemn and reverent, they
repeated the words: "If either should die,
and spirits may come back from heaven, that
will we do, that the grave may be robbed of
its terror, and death be robbed of its sting.
Still living and loving we'll comfort the
other with help and advice from above,
awaiting with patience and calmness and
hope the time that shall see us united."

This said, their hearts got rid of the burden
of care and deep gloom which oppressed
them, and Ruth, with a smile, half of love,
half contrition, said low in a whisper to
Philip: "I'm ashamed of my fears, but remember, whenever death may divide us,

we'll think of our vow, and maintain the compact quite sacred."

The autumn had come, with a breath of the north, painting with artistic fancy the leaves of the trees and mosses and ferns with patches of russet and yellow. The jessamine and clematis, climbing the porch, were resplendent with crimson and gold, as though they had stolen some fire from the sun, when he lingered to kiss them " Good evening." The fruits were all ripe, and the harvest was in ; the farmers rejoiced at the plenty. The sun still shone brightly, but the wind it grew cool, and came through the trees as though sobbing. The souls of the trees were grieved for the pain, and shed golden tears in their sorrow, till the ground was strewn with heaps of brown leaves, which the wind, in its wild gusty passion, whirled high in the air, then twisted round, and scattered them over the meadows. The mosses crept down from the trunks of the trees, till the gnarled rugged bark was left naked. The squirrels sat solemnly eating their nuts among the few leaves still remaining, a-trembling with cold as the breeze

swept along; so they made up their mind
that winter was near, and scampered away
to their dwellings. The birds had gone southwards looking for summer; only sparrows
and robins were left to cogitate over the
ways and the means, or to converse with
grave speculation on the truth of the proverb,
that winters were long when the hips and
the haws were in plenty; for the hips and
the haws gleamed ruddy and bright on bare
hedges of wildrose and hawthorn.

The Mill Stream 'neath the trees looked
sulky and sad, as though vexed with having
to carry the burden of leaves, which the wild
wind had hurried down from the trees and
the roadside. The wind grew colder and
wilder and stronger, the rain came down in
torrents. The birds took shelter in cranny
and nook, and sleepily said to each other,
"It is wiser to stay with our heads under
our wings, than to go hopping about in such
weather." The storms grew wilder, and more
frequent and longer; but at last they ceased
altogether. But nothing was left of the
leaves of the trees, nor ferns, nor mosses,
nor flowers; not a sound could be heard but

the voice of the stream, or the chirping of obins or sparrows.

Then down fell the snow, and covered the earth in a garment of heavenly whiteness. One might almost have thought that the spring-time had come, and the trees had been laden with blossoms. The snow was so fair, so pure, that angels themselves up in heaven might have envied the homes of the mortals below and rejoiced in its fairness and beauty. Only the Mill Stream looked angry and grim, as blackly it hurried along, winding its sinuous way through the fields, like the serpent that crept into Eden.

The winter had come, and Ruth's heart it grew light, for Philip had said in a letter that, in spite of the frost, the snow, or the cold, they should spend a sweet Christmas together. Her eyes grew bright, for her heart was light, and with gladness was running over. Her voice ever raised in a song of sweet praise for the love and the blessings around her. So swiftly the time of his absence had passed, preparing the clothes for the wedding, that in spite of the longing for Christmas to come, the days

seemed too short for their labour. But
now all was ready, and in the old church
their names had been " called " by the parson.
Nothing had happened, and Philip was well,
and Ruth had all fears nigh forgotten.
Bright and gay as a bird, she carroled and
sang, a-filling the old house with music, till
the robins themselves closed their little black
eyes, and their heads set to one side to listen.

'Twas the even of Christmas; the work
was all done, the miller was home from the
mill. Ruth's heart it beat high at every
strange sound; her cheek it was crimson
with blushes, as her father would give a
sly glance at her face, and whisper, " Surely
this is him coming." The snow had been
falling, but now it had ceased, and all the
bright stars were a-shining; and through the
bare branches of trees by the stream the
new silver moon was a-peeping. The air
it was frosty and cutting and keen; the
icicles hung from the housetops, or clung
to the trees and the stones and the hedges,
a-glinting and gleaming like jewels. Im-
patient and restless, Ruth stood by the door,
unheeding the cold wintry weather. Surely

never before were horses so slow or coaches
so tardy a-coming. "Mother, give me my
hood; I'll run down the lane, for I'm certain
that something has happened."

The miller looked up with a smile at his
wife, and she laughed as she glanced at her
daughter. Ruth blushed, turned away with
the hood on her head, paused just for a
moment to listen; then hearing the sound of
the coach on the road, she glanced once more
in at the kitchen. It all looked so cosy, so
home-like and warm; the table was spread;
her parents were sitting close by the fire,
he reading, she knitting, both waiting the
coming of Philip. Ruth's heart swelled with
love for her parents and home; just then in
her heart they stood brightest. Turning back
to the chair where her father was seated, she
curled his white locks round her fingers;
turning them round and round, till at last his
neck with her arm she encircled; and drop-
ping her head to his cheek, she kissed him,
lingering, waiting, yet wanting to go. A
feeling momentous possessed her. "Will
you not come too, to the end of the lane?"
she said in the ear of the miller. But her

father just laughed : " No, no, I'm too old to
expose my limbs to the frost and the cold, for
I'm not in love with young Philip." So Ruth
laughing lightly, ran out of the house, saying
brightly : " I'll stop just ten minutes."

The minute-hand of the old kitchen clock
just pointed ten minutes to seven ; but Philip
arrived ere it chimed out the hour, and all
the first greetings were over. " Where is
Ruth ?" he asked, after waiting awhile for the
sound of her voice or her footsteps. " Where
is Ruth ?" for he missed the sweet " Welcome," for which all the day he'd been longing. " Where is Ruth ? ' " Ah ! she went
out to meet you, I wonder that you did not
see her ; but she will not be long ; she said
she'd be back in ten minutes."

Ten minutes, twenty, an hour had passed
by, and still no signs of returning. They
sought the lane through, from the house to
the village, over hill, over dale, over meadows.
The whole of the villagers turned out that
night, with shouts and lanterns to find her.
But all was in vain ; no trace of the maiden
was found. In tearless anguish the mother
prayed for some voice from heaven to guide

them. But no voice replied, not a sound could be heard, e'en the voice of the Mill Stream was silent, for the ice on its surface was creeping. Only the cries of the searchers were heard, as they echoed all over the valleys.

The morning of Christmas dawned brightly and clear, but all was woe in the village. No dinners were eaten, no sermons were preached, for the pastor himself had said to them, with tears in his eyes and trembling tones : "It is better to work than be talking."

And he worked with the men who, with shovels and spades, every heap of the snow did turn over. From daylight till darkening they delved and they dug, but never a sign of the maiden. Then torches they made them, and worked by their light, although they knew well if they found her life would be flown, and 'twas only the clay they could give to the arms of the mother. But Philip's pale face, her mother's sad moans, and the noiseless grief of the miller, spurred them on in their work, and they felt no fatigue, till at last no spot was left covered where either a fox or a hare could have hidden. One by one, slowly, they gave

up the search, and returned to their homes
in the village.

To the house, with the miller, the parson
returned, and endeavoured with Christian
patience to bring consolation and calmness
where all now was woe and lamenting. It
is hard to believe that all works for good,
when nothing but evil is present; so they
thought and they felt, when he prayed
them to say: "Whatever Thou doest, O
Lord, it is good; for Thy mercy endureth
for aye." "We know," said the pastor,
his eyes streamed as he spoke, for Ruth
was to him as a daughter. "We know
the great wonders He works for our good,
and in all things a blessing is hidden.
Who knows what a joy may come out of
affliction, though in this case at present 'tis
hid? Yet, sometimes, when peace has
softened your hearts, a gleam of bright joy
may come to you, borne of this very affliction. Great troubles come to us, but while
we are brooding, and black melancholy sits
still in our hearts, a star shines through
the clouds; at first 'tis but small, but ere
long it illumines the darkness, and we bask

in the light and rejoice in the brightness,
forgetting the clouds, and loving the light
better, because we at first had the darkness. The darkness is round you to-day;
well I know it; have faith in God and His
goodness. If Ruth has gone, 'tis but a
while; you too will go sometime to join
her. Think how brightly for you that
morning will dawn, when, after the pain
and the sorrow, you close your eyes on the
earth below, and join your loved daughter
in heaven. And you, brother Philip, is
your faith so weak that you need me to
tell you your duty? You preach to your
people the goodness of God, the need of
faith and submission. Where is your faith?
Can it not sustain you, and help you to
bear this affliction? God has thought fit to
lay His hand heavily on you, to chasten and
teach you, to make you more humble. In love
hath He done it, for those whom He loves
doth He chasten. Bend down to the yoke
and wear it, with faith, on your shoulders."

"'Tis easy to talk," said Philip, "of faith:
I have, and thought I possessed it. Yet
now, when I need it, I find it a word

empty and devoid of meaning. When she stood beside me my faith was unbounded; this life, the next, all eternity opened before me. Not a doubt or a fear overshadowed my mind. Ruth lived; my knowledge of that gave me a foundation to build on. I loved God all the better, because I loved her, because she lived and loved me. She is dead, and for ever, as far as I know, I never again shall behold her. The future is black to my eyes as the starless midnight of winter. And I know that I never had faith. I was only happy in knowledge; taking for granted all that was preached, not using my reason; contented to hang my hopes upon others' talk; think, act, as did others. Now all is changed; when I need faith I find it is wanting. You are older than I am—help me to find it; give me something to hold on. Give me proof that my darling is sleeping; that she will some day awake, and my eyes shall behold her, as though nothing had happened to part us. Do you know it for certain? Say you do. I'll believe you. I know you're a good man and true. If you know it, oh help me to learn it as well. Teach me faith, teach me life is immortal!"

With horror the old man looked down on his friend, his friend whom he thought almost saintly. "God help you, my brother! I fear that I cannot. No faith! Ah, how can I help you? Faith cannot be taught, it comes of itself, a breath from the angels in heaven. It comes not by logic, nor reason, nor thought, it is inspiration from heaven."

It was the day that had been set for the wedding; the sun had gone to its rest. The house was still; its inmates slept—all slept, save Philip; he alone was awake. The old folks, weary with grief, had gone to their beds, entreating him to do likewise. Still he sat by the fire with gloomy eyes fixed on its embers, watching the flickering lights gleam and then expire anon to rise up more brightly.

Unconscious his thoughts, which erstwhile had been fixed on his troubles, were turned and absorbed by the fanciful shapes of the embers. Two flames danced together, now rising, now falling, now steady, now waving, but always keeping together, and, childlike, he named them—one Ruth and one Philip;

and he watched them intently, feeling strange
interest in every movement; Philip the
larger, more steady and stable, Ruth, smaller
and brighter, more waving. Like a child
he endowed them with fictitious life, weaving
a future before them, as once he had woven
for Ruth and himself; when, crash! falls
the coal with so sudden a sound, he starts
from his seat with a groan. Remorseful,
his thoughts from his troubles had wavered,
to weave such pictures fantastic. When again
he glanced at the fire, the flame he called
Ruth was lost in the blackness of coal; not
a spark nor a gleam of it left. Ruth was
dead, the light from the embers had fallen;
only the flame he called Philip was left.

Again his wandering fancy endowed it with
being; he watched it quiver and tremble,
and hang o'er the blackness into which the
other had fallen. And he bitterly said to
himself: "So must my life be henceforward,
striving with vain endeavour to pierce the
darkness before me; to see beyond death
and the grave which engulfed her; longing
myself to die, and solve the mystery, yet
clinging to life, and fearing the end of

L

existence, fearing that this is the whole, and the end to be found in the graveyard. How can I preach life immortal to men, when I myself cannot believe it! O God! give me faith! nay more, give me knowledge; grant me one inspiration from heaven. Not for myself do I ask it alone, but for those who call me their teacher. Send light in my darkness! O God! give me truth to lighten the burden of others!"

So he prayed, and he wrestled, like Jacob of old, for knowledge and wisdom to guide him. His breast was torn with conflicting emotions; with grief for his loss and gloomy forebodings, distrust for the future, remorse for the past, doubts and fears of the life everlasting. Long he fought, long he prayed, as one fighting a battle that ends either in life or in death; till worn out and weary, his strength all exhausted, from weakness itself a calmness came o'er him; and he sobbed as a child sobs to sleep, and he dreamed.

He dreamed that a bright form came near him with looks full of love and compassion, that soft tender hands were laid light on his brow! And, lifting his head from his bosom, he saw the figure of Ruth there beside him! his Ruth, as of yore, though strangely trans-figured, and light with heavenly radiance. Was he mad? Was he dreaming? Did his eyes not deceive him? Was it really his darling beside him, or had reason deserted its throne? He gasped for breath, with an agonised cry, his hands outstretched in appealing: "Ruth! Ruth! is it you? 'tis not madness, not dreaming? oh, speak! my heart hungers to hear you!"

Then accents familiar fell soft on his ear, words of love and tender compassion, of warning, of teaching, and gentle upbraiding, bidding him master his grief and go forth on his mission: "Teach men their duty to God, and themselves; teach mercy and kindness and goodness of heart, to bear with the failing of others. Teach them they are the seed in the garden of earth, that must afterward open in heaven. Nay more—teach them this—that every vile thought, bad action, or vicious desire, will rest like a blight on the seed, and canker-like eat of its substance till only the heart of it is left,— the life which no worm can destroy. Then, when this life is done, and the seed is removed, the work of the earth-life is wasted in sorrow, in pain, in useless remorse, vain regrets, and wearying longings. The work must be done that on earth was neglected, every sin be atoned that once was committed; not by repentance alone, but by work, as one who has builded a house, and finds its foundation unsteady, finds it vain to endeavour by building it higher to make it more safe and secure; the whole superstructure must come to the ground, the fault rooted out and repaired. If the seed be not good, then the plant must be stunted and weak in its growing. Cheer them on in their troubles, help them carry their burdens; tell them the lost ones still live and hover about them; tell them they die not, nor sleep not, but ever are waiting to help them, with love and with sympathy, longing to greet them not far away, but just by a veil separated, trying to guide them, and urge them with beckoning finger, onwards, into the regions of knowledge and light."

So she talked, and he listened, not daring to speak, while into his soul came a calmness as came on the waves of Galilee's sea, when the voice of the Lord had said, "Peace!"

Many wondered thereafter, who looked on his face, and said: "He was not greived to lose her," for the light had returned to his eyes; to his cheek had come back the colour. But his voice it was softer, his manner more mild, forbearing and gentle. Grief had all vanished, hope dwelt in its place, and faith that had come there by knowledge.

When the winter was over and springtime had come, the ice and the snow had all melted; then they found what they sought—the body of Ruth—that lay 'neath the rushing mill-waters. Then those that were watching him say a few tears crept down his cheek, but he smiled to himself as he said, "Not lost, only changed, yet ever my own, my teacher, my helper, my friend."

Since then years have flown. The miller has gone, and his wife, full of years, rejoicing, has joined him. Only Philip is left, an old man and grey, with the burden of years on his shoulders; a seed almost ripe for the planting. In his church on a Sabbath, he preaches to men, tells them of the life everlasting.

Right dearly they love him, the kindly old man, whose life to their good is devoted. To him in their troubles come children and men, and make him their father confessor; tell him their follies and trials, and feeling the better because of the love that he bears them. Their burdens grow light when he, with kind sympathy, helps them. 'Tis said in a whisper, that when all is still, he talks with the spirits from heaven; that the spirit of Ruth ever waits by his side; young Ruth, who was drowned in the stream. Some say they have seen her, some say they have heard her, conversing in soft tones with Philip. But they love him no less, but rather the more, that he holds close communion with heaven.

He teaches the doctrine of love to the world, he frights not with terror and darkness. "God is love" is the creed that he teaches; and further—that, as all men from God are forthcoming, and ever to God are returning, their lives and their actions, every one, should be to His honour and glory.

There he lives in the house by the stream; the Mill-Stream they call it, for a little higher there stands the remains of a mill. And through it comes rushing, the stream, whirring and churring along, making strange sounds as it goes; but no longer the wheels and machinery turn, nor the stones revolve, as in the days of the miller of old; the mill is deserted, and another is built where the corn is ground for the farmers. Still the stream goes roaring and foaming; twisting and turning and clashing, twirling and curling and eddying round, as though in vexation of spirit; splashing and crashing and rushing along, with a dash and a roar like the distant verberation of thunder.

Lower down it widens and opens into a lagoon, bordered with larches and willows. It smiles in the air of the heavens, reflecting the glory of sunlight. Peaceful and smooth is its surface, undisturbed by the tumult above it. Calm and serene, it flows gently along towards the end of the journey. Peaceful and happy, content with its lot and its station. Like one who has passed through the troubles of life; experienced all of life's evils—overcome them; and now, content with his work, is gliding along to the haven.

"THEN Fraulein does not believe in ghosts?"

No, the Fraulein did not, and said so. Moreover, she had a distinct opinion that the subject was not one suitable to the occasion.

They were standing in a recess, shaded by flowering shrubs and palms, from the other side of which came the murmur of voices.

She had chosen to sit out this dance for two reasons, the first being that she had caught an intelligent gleam in a pair of honest dark eyes, as she had whirled by on the arm of her partner, in the last waltz, and the interpretation thereof brought an answering light to her own grey orbs, and a flush to her cheek.

The second reason was, that the man whose name was written against the next dance did not please her fastidious taste, so she had pleaded fatigue and begged to be excused. "I will sit here," she said, "and rest; but you, Herr Lieutenant, must not lose this dance, I shall be quite well alone."

To her chagrin the Herr Lieutenant seemed as pleased to sit out the dance as she herself, and with a bow took a seat beside her. Fraulein Naumann's face clouded with ill-concealed vexation, which her partner must have perceived, had not his senses been dulled by the copious draughts of wine in which he had indulged. He did not notice that her gaze was turned expectantly in the direction of the doorway, as she answered his platitudes absently, with an air of boredom.

The murmur of voices on the other side of the palms grew more distinct as the music of the band died away. A little group of persons were discussing some subject, in which belief or non-belief in ghosts and supernatural agencies figured largely, and the two lapsed into silence and listened.

She was wishing with all her heart that he would go and leave her, but the interest he took in their neighbours' conversation made him blind to the coolness of her attitude towards him. Moreover, there was something about her—a sense of calm steadiness and strength—which gave him an odd feeling of security. He felt himself safer and stronger in her presence, and he was glad of an excuse to remain beside her.

"It's queer how these stories of ghosts crop up now and again!" he remarked. Then seeing she did not reply, he continued, "Of course nobody really believes in them, but they have a sort of hold on one somehow. One finds one's self interested in spite of one's disbelief. Is it not so with you, Fraulein?"

"Not at all," she replied coldly. "It is a subject that has no interest for me." Then feeling she had answered a little rudely she added, "You see, Herr Lieutenant, I have been educated in too sensible a school, and kept too busily occupied with my work, to have time to spend over so unprofitable a subject as ghost lore."

"That one might expect of the clever daughter of Professor Naumann; still, my Fraulein, there are many clever men who do not think the study of ghost lore unprofitable, if one can believe what one reads."

" That is not saying much for their common sense, in spite of their reputation. I know there are many stories of supernatural appearances believed in, but in my opinion they are founded on some easily explained occurrence, and added to by the imaginations of the various narrators. I feel sure if one had time and inclination to look into, and get to the root of these stories, they would be found to have no real foundation."

" Perhaps you are right with respect to many of the stories, but so many really sensible folks believe in the possibility of spirit return, that one does not know what to think."

" That is just it," she retorted scornfully. " It is less trouble to believe in other peoples' belief instead of thinking for one's self. If a man is reputed clever, he will find any number of others ready to adopt his fantasies, and swear to them as proven facts."

" On the principle of one fool makes many, you think ?"

" Yes, if you like to put it in that way. But do you believe in ghosts, Herr Lieutenant ?" she asked abruptly, turning her eyes a little contemptuously on his face. It was evident, even to him, that her opinion of his common sense was not a high one.

"I—no—that is—I've never seen one, but I fancy I should believe in them if ever I did."

"If ever you did. Yes, but you never will, Herr Lieutenant."

"It would give you a creepy sensation to turn a corner and come suddenly on some one you knew was dead; don't you think so?"

"It might act so on some people," she rejoined with some impatience, "but I have no superstitious fears to begin with, and should know at once that some one was playing a trick on me, or that my eyes deceived me."

"And you would not be afraid?"

"No! why should I? Our conversation is a curious one—let us talk of something else; or you can get me an ice or something."

"Then, my Fraulein, let us make a bargain—you and I." He was very loath to leave her, and ignored her evident attempts to get rid of him.

" A bargain ? "

" Yes ! It is this ! If I should happen to die first, I will come and see you, if you will allow me ; then we will see whether you or those friends behind the palms are right."

" You will have to come in some extraordinary and unmistakable fashion then," she laughed ; " not in the orthodox white sheet."

" You give me leave to come then, if I can ? "

" Oh yes ! and welcome ; I am not afraid. But you are not thinking of leaving this world yet, Herr Lieutenant ? "

" No ! oh no ! only one never knows, of course, what may happen. War may break out, or a hundred other things occur, any of which might end one's short existence here."

He had her dance programme in his hand, and was busily inscribing something on the back. He did not see the sudden flush and brightening of her face, as the curtain was pushed aside and a young man entered, nor the meaning glance which passed between a pair of dark and a pair of grey eyes.

"This is our dance, Fraulein," said the new-comer; "shall we go?"

The young lady rose, and held out her hand for her programme. The Lieutenant hung it by the silken cord over her wrist, and bowed.

"Thanks, very much, my Fraulein. I have made a note of the engagement on the back, and I shall not forget." He bowed again, and stood moodily tugging at his moustache, watching the two take their places in the dance, she with a look on her face that somehow caused a feeling of bitterness in his heart, and then with a shrug of the shoulders he turned and sought the refreshment-room.

CHAPTER II

IT was the old story. Betting, billiards, wine, women. A few years of wild excess—feverish pursuit of pleasure, and elusive joys, and then the end—a suicide's grave, a lunatic's straight jacket, a criminal's cell, or a wretched, poverty-stricken, disgraceful old age. Lieutenant Harald Arnhult had chosen the lot of the suicide, and now lay on his bed with a bullet in his brain. The bespattered walls of his room gave evidence of how it had come there.

The local newspapers of Stuttgart had given the news and the manner of his death to the townspeople that morning, affording a subject for conversation among those who had called themselves his friends, or those who had been familiar with the handsome dissipated face of the man who now lay dead in the room, mercifully darkened to hide the dreadful sight from the light of day.

Friends he had but few. There had been plenty who had called themselves his friends, among whom he had daily spent hours of his time, at the card-table, the billiard-room, or at the cafés, where the waitresses were the recipients of their gallantries and wine-soddened admiration.

To-day the friends were to be found in the same haunts, discussing—cue or wine-glass in hand—the news conveyed to them by the daily papers, of the fate of one of their number. They knocked the ivory balls about, emptied their glasses, and told little questionable anecdotes of him. His extravagance was commented on, the amount of his debts calculated, but no word of sorrow or regret for the young life wasted. Apparently there was no thought given to the warning of what the future might hold for themselves.

He was gone! Better both for himself and for them that he had taken himself out of the way, before he had brought down further disgrace upon them all! There might have been another way out of the difficulty; he might have married a rich woman, and with her money have cleared his way; but he was always a fool!

The balls clicked, the scores ran high, stakes were won and lost, glasses were filled, emptied and refilled again and again, and into the still small hours the game went merrily on, while he, who had the night before played as merrily as the rest and now lay dead, was scoffed at as a fool and a coward.

Yes! he had been a fool, and sooner or later *a fool must pay for his folly.*

In the house in Kaiser Wilhelms-strasse
the dead man lay, waiting his dishonoured
grave. In a room on the floor above him—
the floor occupied by Professor Naumann and
his family—some ladies were sitting drinking afternoon tea, and condoling with the
lady of the house on the unpleasant occurrence so near to her.

"Such a horrid affair! dear Frau Professor.
I felt so sorry for you when I heard the
news. That's the worst of these town houses;
one is so frequently brought in contact with
one's neighbours. One can scarcely avoid
meeting them sometimes, and, in such a
case as this, it must be most unpleasant
for you."

"Yes, it is very sad!" replied the Frau
Professor, whose kindly face showed traces
of tears. "It gave me a great shock. My
boys and girls used to know him so well.
They were good friends, and he used to
be in and out with them, till he got in
with that fast set, and turned so wild. I
feel terribly grieved; he was a nice boy
even then, but I had my boys to think of,
and so——"

The worthy Frau Professor dried a tear that fell upon her plump cheek, and the sentence remained unfinished.

Yes; she had had her own sons to think of, and was afraid of the companionship of the lad who had begun to tread the downward path. Afraid of the temptation for her own, but, thank God! her boys were good, and she could afford to shed a pitiful tear for that other mother's son, who lay dead in the room below, the manner of whose death bore witness to the ruined, wasted life.

"I thought at one time he was a little fond of your eldest daughter," remarked the visitor.

"Did you? I don't think so. I never noticed anything. They met now and then —after he had ceased to come in and out as a schoolboy—at dances and such like; but Gertrude was never inclined for flirting or much gaiety. She was always taken up with her studies, and seldom cared to leave them for such amusements as girls generally love. We were afraid she would never marry, but now that she is betrothed, and her marriage arranged, I hope she will give up her ideas of a profession and independent life."

"When are your daughters returning home?"

"Before the end of the year. There is so much to do before the wedding. Gertrude must give up her studies, and help with the preparations. Mina comes too, so I shall have all my children at home again for a while. The little ones are looking forward with delight to their sister's home-coming."

So the conversation drifted into other channels. The faults, failings, and fate of the dead man were forgotten in the discussion of the more important topics of wedding presents, wedding gowns, and wedding bells.

A few weeks later there was great joy in the Naumann household. The professor and his kindly wife were rejoicing in the home-coming of their daughters. Nor were the girls themselves less happy to be under the parental roof. In spite of the triumphs scored and honours won at the seat of learning, Gertrude had bidden farewell to

her youthful dreams of fame and independence, and was looking forward to a future
spent together with one for whom she
thought the world, fame, and independence
well lost.

It was a warm summer night, when the
sisters, having repaired to their room, sat
near the open window, eagerly discussing
and recounting what had passed since last
they had been together. They had both
been away from home some six months, and
there was much to tell and to hear.

The girls lingered long over their preparations for the night, the excitement of home-
coming drove sleep from their eyes. A
flickering of the candles caused them to look
up, and Mina rose to close the window, when
her sister uttered a strange, horrified cry. At
the same instant she saw a sight which held
her rooted to the floor. A man had put aside
the fluttering curtains and stepped into the
room !

Mina sprang to her sister's side, and
together they stood facing the intruder. For
an instant they stood looking at each other;
then Mina, with a shuddering sob, gasped,

"It's Harald Arnhult," and hid her face on her sister's breast.

Gertrude stood still, though with wildly beating heart. Her lips seemed stiff as though turned to stone, but recovering herself with a mighty effort, she said, "Is it you, Harald Arnhult, or is it a trick to frighten us?"

The man seemed to try to speak, his lips moved, but no sound came.

"Whoever you are," said Gertrude, "go now!"

The man bowed his head, and in that gesture was expressed a pitiful submission that brought a pang to the girl's heart.

"It is Harald Arnhult," whispered Mina, raising her head. "Are you not happy?" she asked in trembling tones, still clinging to her sister.

It seemed for a moment that an agonized smile played over his face—a smile that made Mina cover her eyes, with a cry. Then he turned slowly towards the still open window, and was gone.

The girls darted to the window and looked down into the quiet street. It was deserted.

The moonlight brought out in detail the windows and doorways of the houses opposite, the flowers and plants on the small balconies fluttering in the night breeze. But no trace of human form was seen, or sound of steps was heard to break the silence.

For some time the girls stood looking down from the window, till, with a moaning cry, Mina turned to her sister. "O Gertrude! Gertrude! what does it mean?"

Gertrude was silent, but her thoughts had flown back to that conversation in the ball-room nearly a year ago. She had not thought of it again, but now she remembered, with almost painful distinctness, every word that had passed between them, her scornful impatience of the subject, and the feeling of almost pitying aversion she had felt for the young man, whose wine and tobacco-laden breath she had tried to avoid. As she remembered, a pang of remorse for this feeling swept over her. He had seemed so much in earnest, and she—well, she had only wanted him to leave her, to make room for that other for whom she waited.

These thoughts crowded into her memory

and she replied, "I think I know what it means."

Her sister looked inquiringly into her face. "Tell me," she whispered.

"You remember the night of the ball at the general's house?"

"Yes, it was the night you became engaged!"

Gertrude nodded. "I was to dance with Harald Arnhult, but excused myself, for I had promised to wait for that dance and sit it out with Max; but Lieutenant Arnhult would not leave me. There were some people behind, talking of ghosts, and he took up the subject. He had been drinking, and could not see that I did not want him. Then Max came. Harald Arnhult wrote something on my programme about coming to see me after he was dead. I did not pay any attention to it, for, as I tell you, he had been drinking wine and I thought him stupid. I went away with Max, and I never saw Lieutenant Arnhult again."

While speaking, Miss Naumann had been hastily turning over a little litter in an open drawer. "Ah, here it is!" she said, drawing forth a little gilt-edged card with a white silken cord attached, and examining the pencilled lines on the flowered back, she read—

> "Mem. Engaged to pay a post-mortem visit to Miss Gertrude Naumann, in such fashion —not orthodox—as will remove her doubts as to the possibility of spirit return.
>
> "Signed this 3rd day of October, at 11.30 P.M., in the ball-room of General S.'s house in Stuttgart.
>
> "HARALD ARNHULT."

The tears blinded the eyes of the frightened, awe-stricken Mina as she read, and sobbed "Poor Harald Arnhult!"

"Poor Harald Arnhult!" repeated Gertrude, as with shaking hands she laid the card back in the drawer.

It was not long before it began to be rumoured abroad that the home of the Naumann family in Kaiser Wilhelms-strasse was haunted by the ghost of the lieutenant who had committed suicide in the rooms below. There were those who said that he not only haunted the house, but was a familiar and expected guest, that he might be seen in drawing-room, dining-room, or study, wherever the family were assembled.

"This is terrible," remarked a frightened lady one day to the Frau Professor. "Why do you not remove from the house? Can the clergyman do nothing to rid you of this awful thing? They used to exorcise evil spirits, you know. Why do you not let something of the kind be tried?"

"He is no evil spirit," said Gertrude, answering for her mother; "only poor unhappy Harald Arnhult, sinful enough, and weak enough, but no worse than he was, only more miserable, more unhappy, because he knows of the terrible mistake he made, and cannot undo. He can, or will, not do us any harm, and if it makes him happier to come to us, why should we drive him away?"

"But the children! He will frighten them to death. Your nurse told me how he had come into the nursery and they had screamed themselves almost into fits."

"Yes!" replied the Frau Professor, "they were dreadfully frightened, for they remembered him, of course, but we remonstrated with

him, and told him not to go into the nursery
or frighten the children, and he promised he
would not. Since then he has not done so."

"Well, I should have died had such a
thing happened in my home. I cannot
think how you can take it so calmly."

"We are becoming used to see him, and,
in fact, look for him, and he seems pleased
and grateful to us for tolerating his presence. I sometimes wish we had been
kinder to him when he lived among us
He had no mother, you know, and that
makes a difference to a young man." .

"But, dear Frau Professor, what can it
lead to? What can be the end of it?
What is the meaning of it?"

"Nay, I cannot tell, but God knows."

Some time later, a party of friends met
at the railway station to take leave of the
family of the professor, who were intending
to make a holiday at the seaside. The children, in wild spirits at the release from the
schoolroom, and the prospect of unlimited
freedom from books and lessons, laughed and
shouted with glee as the train came thun-
dering up to the platform. The guard un-

locked the door of the compartment reserved for them, and the youngsters climbed in.

"There's somebody there already," remarked one of the assembled friends, indicating a gentleman seated in the farthest corner.

"Yes, but it's only Lieutenant Arnhult, and we know him," answered the child.

The professor, his wife, and daughters, took their places and waved their adieus to their waiting friends, and the train moved out of the station, leaving the little group standing on the platform staring after it.

"Did you see him?" asked one gentleman at length, turning to his companions.

"Yes, I saw him; there was no mistake —he was plain enough to be seen."

"But what do you make out of it?"

"I—I can make nothing out of it, but it seems to me that Shakespeare was right when he made that remark about there being more things in heaven and earth than are dreamt of in our philosophy. I cannot attempt to explain it, but that man in the carriage was Harald Arnhult, and after that I can be satisfied that there is more than mere rumour in the affair in Kaiser Wilhelms-strasse."

HE lay on the straw mattress of his bed, with dulled eyes turned longingly to the tiny window, through which he watched the sinking sun gilding the stems of the pine trees, turning them to red gold, and sending shafts of glorious light between the trunks on to the soft moss that covered the ground beneath them.

Away in the distance, the same radiance lay over the fields, where the rye stood in sheaves like an army; over the meadowlands, over the purple moors where the wild birds had built their nests, over the rugged hills in the distance, clothing their nakedness in the royal garments of purple, and crimson, and gold.

The buzz of myriad insects was in the air, and occasionally the chirp of a bird, or the chatter of a flighty squirrel, reached his ear, as he lay drinking in the beauty of the evening hour.

Then, from the branches of a birch tree that swept the roof of the hut, came a rich burst of melody, as a nightingale sang its hymn of love and longing. The sound caught the ear of the dying man, and he raised himself painfully from his hard pillow to listen. Low and clear rose the rich notes on the balmy air, quivering in sweet, soft cadence, then burst triumphantly into a very ecstasy of jubilant song, scattering gems of sweet sounds over the sun-bathed earth, which sent back its thanks in a thousand soft perfumes, that rose like incense to the singer. Then the music grew soft and low, the notes fuller and longer, trembling with sweet, sad melancholy, that rose and fell like waves of the sea, and floated away, away over the glowing fields and waving meadows, and the thoughts of the man followed where they led him. Away, away over the hills, into the golden haze, to the Land of Long-ago; where the trees grew taller, the hills higher, where the skies were brighter, the sunshine more golden, the days

longer, the nights darker and more fearsome
—a land more full of mystery and wonder
than any other.

There he saw two children at play, the
one strong and sturdy, bearing himself with
a valiant air, proud of his strength and
courage to protect the other, who walked
by his side and clung to his hand. Now
chasing the butterflies, now wandering in the
scented woods, gathering the ripe luscious
berries ; or, in the winter, flying a-down the
hillside on a rough-hewn sledge, he steering
the course of the flying steed, and she con-
fiding in his strength and skill.

Still together, hand in hand, going to and
fro to school, learning from the same torn
and well-thumbed primer, painfully helping
each other to spell the long words, whose
meanings were so hard to understand. Singing the same songs, playing the same merry
games, listening to the rush of waters, when
the melting snows filled the streams to over-
flowing, and went rushing, dancing, and
swirling over their feet when they would
cross to the other side on the stepping-
stones.

"Wait for me!" she called, as he with bared feet stepped into the chilly water.

"I will go first, and try if it is safe—be patient till I come to fetch you."

So he went first, setting his feet cautiously on the slippery stones, trying each one. Then he came back to fetch her—she half-laughing, half-weeping, in her fear to be swept away, but he, brave and sturdy, lifting her in his strong young arms and bearing her safely over, setting her down on the other side.

He followed them on and on—to the sun-lit woods, where the white stems of the birches showed like fair ladies, in delicate fluttering draperies of tender green, amid the stately pines that rose, straight and sombre, to the blue heavens. He heard the murmur of the evening breeze among their branches, and the pit-a-patter, pit-a-patter of the birch leaves, as they whispered to each other of a secret they knew.

Then a stronger breeze in mischievous frolic lifted the sweeping draperies that hid a moss-grown stone, and revealed a youth and maiden, whose wandering steps had brought them to that enchanted wood, where only they and love exist.

Then, still hand in hand, they arose, and with happy hearts followed the dancing, gleaming light, that Hope held out before them. They pressed on joyfully, leaving the Land of Long-ago with its golden glory of sunshine, its rosy mists, that veiled it in sweet soft delicate beauty, and entered the Land of To-day, with its grey clouds and shadows, its toil, its privations, its suffering and pains.

The rising sun called them to labour, the setting sun to rest. Oft-times they were weary, with aching limbs. Oft-times there was not bread for all. Sickness came and times of trial—but still they bore them to-gether—still hand in hand.

Childhood had been left in the Land of Long-ago. The man and woman lived in the Land of To-day; but the light from the Land of Long-ago sometimes helped to brighten the clouds, and, together, they could bear the burden of toil and poverty, cheered by the gleam and the dancing, elusive lamps, that Hope, sweet Hope, still held out before their weary, halting feet.

Always together—always together; and now—the man's feet had brought him to the shores of the river that divides the Land of To-day, from the Land that Is-to-be. And he stood alone. And she——

His restless fingers plucked the coverlet, and rested at last on the bowed head of the weeping woman who knelt by his side, and twined themselves lovingly in the soft tangled hair.

The song of the bird had died away and was silent, the last rays of the setting sun were fading ; but they shed a last glow over the poor couch of the dying man, and over the bowed head of the sobbing woman, half revealing, half hiding the squalor and the poverty that surrounded them. No luxuries, no comforts, not even the necessaries of life were brought to light by the fading gleams ; only hard, bitter poverty, ugliness, and utter bareness. Yet, over the bed, the light shone soft and radiant, and a strain of distant music rose on the air. Was it the last beams of the setting sun ? Was it the refrain of the birds' song ?

The restless fingers paused, and the dying eyes brightened. 'Twas the light from the

N

shores of the Land that Is-to-be, and the man turned his face towards it longingly.

"Wait for me!"—"Wait for me!"

The wailing cry echoed through the sweet sounds of the music, and he hestitated. But the charmed melody drew him on, and the light shone about him, making plain the way.

"Wait for me!" Was it the voice of the child in the Land of Long-ago from the edge of the swollen stream? Or the voice of the woman in the Land of To-day? whose hand drew him back from this other stream he fain would cross, to reach the light and music that lay beyond.

"Wait for me!" The light grew brighter, the music more near.

"I will go first, and see if it is safe; then I will come and fetch you. Do not fear. Let me go. I will come back for you."

With a smile he turned his back on the Land of To-day, and went forward to the Land that Is-to-be; to the light and the sweet sounds of music. And she was left alone.

The sun sank, and rose, and sank again.

The winter came, and covered the mourning earth with its soft white garments. King Frost held the rivers and streams in his iron grasp, and Nature slept. Then came the spring and awakened her, and she rose from her white bed, and dressed herself in garments of tender flower-decked green, to the music of rushing streamlets.

Then followed the summer in golden glory, bringing the promise of plenty in her train, hailed by the music of young birds, and the teaming life of river and field and forest.

Still she waited—patiently waited—till he should come. The day's toil wearied her, for she must toil alone. The night brought little rest, for the hut was lonely and dark, and she was afraid. But she waited, and listened for the sound of his step on the threshold.

He came not! Had he forgotten? Was he content in that land without her?

She smiled even as she asked, for she knew it was not so. He would not forget. He would come to fetch her; but she grew weary with waiting and watching, and longing for his coming.

She tended the grave where they had laid him, in the corner where the dead paupers lay—a resting-place as poor, as bare, as squalid, as their lives had been. But God's rain and sunshine fell on them, and the grass grew soft and green, and flourished above them as bravely as over the rich, where they lay under their marble monuments.

When the toil of the day was done, and sleep fled from her eyes, she would sit there and wait, if perchance he should come there to fetch her.

Eve after eve, the sinking sun left her there. Still he came not.

Then summer passed, and autumn followed in its gorgeously-tinted robes, and purple draperies of shimmering mist.

He had been gone a year. Her feet had grown weary, her eyes dim with watching, her heart faint with longing. And bowing her head on the soft turf, she cried, "Come! Oh come quickly! I cannot bear it longer."

Above her in the chestnut boughs there sounded a soft sweet twitter; then a prelude to the nightingale's song; then a burst of jubilant ecstatic melody, that swelled and throbbed on the air.

A shaft of light fell on the bowed head and spread till it covered her as in a mantle, and covered the grave where she lay. And out of the light he came and took her by the hand; and she rose with a smile of joy ineffable, and followed him out of the darkness, leaving the pain, the sorrow, the toil, and the weariness of the Land of To-day, and hand in hand together they passed on into the glory and light of the Land that Is-to-be.

When the sun rose again, the wondering neighbours found only the worn, toil-wearied body of a woman, who had breathed out her life on the grave of her husband, who had lain down and died a year agone. With pitiful hands they dug a grave, and laid her also to rest beside him, and then went their way, leaving them alone together.

STRANGE EXCURSIONS

Of late years many clever and learned scientists have gone out of their way to demonstrate a fact which William Shakespeare, some three centuries agone, considered beyond dispute.

One of these learned gentlemen—for whom by the way the writer has a great respect—has occupied many years of his life in the conducting of some hundreds of experiments, the results of which, he says, go to prove beyond doubt "that exteriorization of sensibility is a condition possible of accomplishment by hypnotic suggestion, and otherwise."

To many intelligent readers this statement does not convey much meaning, since he has coined the word "exteriorization."

The writer, however, had the advantage of being present at one of the experiments, and was favoured with an oral explanation, as well as an illustration, of the meaning of the mysterious word, which might have suggested something very different from what was actually intended.

Mons. de Rochas, by his experiments, tries to *prove* the facts that man is a twofold being, possessing a material body and a spiritual body; that the material body is entirely dependent on the spiritual body for its existence, but that the spiritual body— even during the life of the material body, by which its movements are hampered and con- fined — can, under certain circumstances, take a holiday as it were, and go off on its own accord, or wander about in search of adventures.

Mons. de Rochas illustrates this theory by sending his subject into a hypnotic sleep, and then he finds, by sticking pins into, or pinching, the air, within a certain distance of the sleeper, that the subject flinches or cries out, as though the pricks or pinches were made upon his person; while if the experi- ment is made on the patient's body itself he gives no sign of sensibility.

It is difficult to see how this proves the

theory of the independent action of the spiritual body, but in some roundabout way Mons. de Rochas thinks it will.

There is a saying that " All roads lead to Rome," and though it would seem that Mons. de Rochas has chosen a very circuitous one, it may be just as safe as the shortest, and possibly some objects of interest may be found on it to beguile the time, till he reaches his destination.

That human beings possess a material body and a spiritual body, was told to man ages and ages ago, but it is the fashion of the hour to be sceptical of all things which have not been tested and proven by our own wisdom and intelligence, in which we place implicit confidence. Faith is nowadays no longer the mode. Men prefer to believe themselves capable of drawing correct inferences and conclusions from their own experiments or arguments, rather than accept the simple statements without palpable demonstration of a long ago dead chronicler.

It is not the writer's province to say they are wrong. Reason, the chiefest glory of man, should be exercised as freely as his limbs; but, in spite of his reasoning powers, man is amazingly shortsighted, and allows much of the proof that he craves for to pass by him unnoticed. Nature lays the keys to her secrets under his very eyes, but he does not see them, and busies himself with what he terms "scientific experiments," to prove a fact which more simple and less learned folk have never doubted.

Without any pretence of proving a theory, or bringing an argument for or against the deductions made by these learned gentlemen, I will relate some incidents, selected from a large number of equal value and interest. Circumstances having proved the truth of these particular cases to be incontrovertible, they are chosen in preference to others, and from them the reader may judge whether the independent action of the spiritual body of still living persons is, or is not, proven.

A gentleman residing in Sweden, much interested in the dairy industry, had for many years been experimenting with milk and its products, with the view of rendering them free from the germs of fermentation.

In these experiments he was assisted by a member of the household, E. E., a lady who carried out his instructions when he, Mr. F., was, for business or other reasons, unable to superintend the work himself.

In 1893 Mr. F. was asked by the principal of a large, well-known dairy firm in Holland, for assistance and advice concerning some difficulty they were in.   As this difficulty was one which had occasioned Mr. F. a good deal of work at different times, and which had been to a great extent overcome, he promised his help, but was prevented by business from undertaking the journey. He proposed that, as E. E. was fully competent to give the required instruction, she should go instead.   Letters were exchanged, and the matter settled ; but the journey was postponed for a week or two, in order that some experiments then on hand might be completed.

It was considered that the results of the microscopical and chemical trials would be useful in illustrating the why and wherefore of the necessity of certain measures to be taken in dealing with the said difficulty.

Mr. F. being away for a few days, his assistant went on with her work of preparing samples for the microscope as well as for the analysts.   In her relation she says :—

" I had several days, with the help of Herr E., worked with the aid of a powerful microscope, without obtaining the conclusion we had expected, viz., that the changes in the different preparations were caused by the development of one particular kind of bacteria.

" Several more days' work in the laboratory, and with the help of the town analyst, was also without any satisfactory result. These failures caused me to suspect that the samples had not been prepared carefully enough, or had not been kept at the temperature which Mr. F. had ordered, but, as I had been compelled to entrust some part of the work to the people at a dairy, I could not be absolutely sure that all the instructions had been faithfully carried out.

" I decided, therefore, that in order to be sure the work was done properly it must be done at a dairy.   For this purpose I wrote to Herr Lamberg—a friend of Mr. F.—who owned a well fitted-up dairy at Bonared, and obtained permission from him to make any use I liked of his dairy, and to consider both it and the assistants at my disposal. I accordingly resolved to go there on the following morning, the 27th October 1893.

"Bonared lies some fifty miles from Gothenburg as the bird flies, but human beings are not supplied with the same means of locomotion, and must needs go a considerably longer way round by train, by steamer, and then by horses and carriage, so that the journey takes some five or six hours to accomplish.

"I had need to be early astir, so made all my preparations before going to bed, and gave orders to be awakened early in the morning, in order to catch the first train.

"The fear of not being called in time kept me awake a good while, but at last I slept, and whilst asleep it seemed to me that I must have set out on my journey, and gone to Bonared. Arrived there, I found nothing had been prepared for my coming, nor were the arrangements such that I could do my work without some alterations. It was necessary that I should have access to the machine-room, as well as liberty to use ice, for the purpose of lowering the temperature of the chamber where my samples must be prepared. This the dairy manager refused point blank, saying that his master had the key of the one, and had given orders that the other must not be touched.

"Irritated and annoyed at the delay thus caused, I make up my mind to seek Herr Lamberg, and get the required permission. Herr Lamberg's residence in Skene is fully five miles from Bonared, but I found myself there at once, dressed in my dairymaid's costume, and with a milk cylinder and thermometer in my hands. How I came there I do not know, neither do I know how I reached Bonared.

"At Skene I asked for Herr Lamberg, but was told I could not see him, as he had not yet left his bedroom.

"I made my way to his room, where at the door I met his wife. I explained to her that it was necessary for me to see her husband without delay, and told her why, but she refused, saying her husband was still asleep, and she would not have him disturbed.

"It seemed to me that Mrs. Lamberg, for some reason or other, was determined I should not speak with him. This new hindrance vexed me, and I made up my mind that I would not be prevented from accomplishing the object of my journey.

"I went into the room, when Mrs. Lamberg again remonstrated angrily at my action. I saw Mr. Lamberg lying in bed, and lifting up his head stared at me with a sort of horrified expression. At this I began to think I had better wait in another room, and sighing over the tiresomeness of the delay, I turned and was passing out, when—the opening of a door aroused me from what had apparently been a profound slumber. It was the servant entering with my morning coffee, and bringing with her a telegram from Mr. F., saying that, as he would be returning home the same day, the journey to Bonared could be put off.

"It was really with difficulty I could persuade myself that my visit to the dairy, and the home of Herr Lamberg, had no other foundation than the baseless fabric of a vision.

I felt as physically tired as though I had actually taken a wearisome journey, and was glad to be able to indulge in another hour's sleep, instead of hurrying to catch a train. This happened on the morning of October 27, 1893, and when Mr. F. returned later in the day, I reported the non-success of our experiment, and told him how my anxiety to get the work done had haunted my sleep the previous night."

The rest of the incident is related by Mr. F., who published the story in a German magazine; he says :—

"A few days later, from 31st October till 2nd November, Herr August Lamberg visited Gothenburg, and called to see me. In the course of conversation he inquired if E. E. was at home, and if she had been recently in his neighbourhood. He was told that she was at home, and had not been away for some time. Whereupon he remarked—

"'It may sound strange to you; in fact, I cannot understand it myself, but I am absolutely certain E. E. was in my house in Skene last Friday. How can she have been at the same time in Gothenburg?'

" ' I cannot pretend to understand it. I can only state what I am convinced is a fact.'

" On being asked for further particulars, Herr Lamberg said—

" ' Last Friday (the 27th October 1893), early in the morning, my wife suddenly awakened me saying, " E. E. is here in the room." When I had fully roused myself, she told me that E. E. had been in the room, but while she (my wife) was awakening me, she had gone out of sight. My wife explained that she had been lying awake, when the door opened and E. E. came in and stood looking at us. She had a large thermometer in her hand. My wife did not understand what E. E. wanted, but judged from the fact of her having a thermometer in her hand that it had something to do with temperature. I of course got up immediately, but found no trace of E. E. in the house. On making further inquiries, my wife said E. E. was wearing a pale print dress, with short sleeves and a white apron. She carried something in one hand which she did not notice particularly, and in the other she held a thermometer.' "

Mrs. Lamberg expressed herself willing, if need be, to declare on oath before the Notary Public that she had seen E. E. at the time and under the circumstances stated. This, however, was not insisted upon, but a document was drawn up which was signed in the presence of three witnesses, testifying to the fact that about four o'clock on the morning of the 27th October 1893, E. E. stood in her chamber in Skene, and that she —Mrs. L.—was fully awake at the time, and recognised her without difficulty.

Mrs. L. added afterwards that E. E.'s appearance did not surprise her as it might otherwise have done, because she was aware of the fact that E. E. intended carrying out some experiments in her husband's dairy at Bonared, but she did not know exactly when.

The witnesses to the document are three of the most respectable persons in Skene, to whom Mrs. Lamberg had told the story the same day it happened.

In further corroboration of the previous statement, and to preclude the possibility of suspicion that it was E. E. herself, in proper person, who was seen by Mrs. Lamberg, a young lady, the foster-daughter of Mr. F., made the following statement :—

"On the evening of 26th October 1893, E. E. decided to go to Bonared to make some experiments, and after having discussed several different matters, and given me some instructions to be carried out, she retired as usual. To my certain knowledge she was in her room next morning, 27th October 1893, from three to seven o'clock, or one hour earlier and three hours after the time she is said to have been seen in Skene. At seven o'clock she drank a cup of coffee."

In concluding this story, an additional note is appended as follows :—

"What is here related are simply the bare facts of the strange incident. I do not offer any explanation. I leave that to others."

Neither does the present writer attempt to explain, though it would seem in this case that the plea of coincidence does not cover the ground.

It might be urged that if in sleep the spirit can visit other scenes and other places, it would be glad to leave such mundane affairs to the care of its material colleague, and seek spheres more in keeping with its spiritual nature.

Who knows? Perhaps it does, but it may be that on its return it can only communicate such details to the material brain as that earthly organ can grasp and understand; that the brain, confined to earth, can understand only such matters as pertain to earth.

But speculation on this subject would open up a vast unexplored land, and I leave the reader to penetrate it for himself.

The next story is not of so commonplace a character, but one likely to become historical.

In the year 1894, a circumstance occurred in the north of Sweden, which, for a very long time, occupied the thoughts of the greater part of the inhabitants of the whole country, and exercised the minds of the cleverest judges and juries for several months. The occurrence in question was the death of a man called Johansson, and the peculiar circumstances that attended it.

Johansson had lived the commonplace life of an ordinary business man, of whose existence probably very few outside of his own little circle were aware. He was accustomed to buy and sell timber, to act as agent for the peasants round about in the disposal of the woods and forests which they owned, to arrange sales, make contracts with the owners of sawmills for the delivery of certain quantities of timber, and was considered a capable man of business.

A good deal of money passed through his hands at different times, as, for instance, when he received payment for the timber floated down the rivers in the spring to the various sawmills. It was on one of these occasions, when he was going north by train with bundles of bank notes in a leathern case, that he was found by the guard of the train lying on the seat of the carriage, to all appearance fast asleep. The guard did not disturb him till the train stopped at the station where Johansson was to alight, and then, when trying to arouse him, he was horror-struck to discover that it was no ordinary slumber, but the sleep of death.

There was no sign of any disturbance; there was no other passenger in the compartment; and the guard had passed and re-passed him several times during the journey, and had seen nothing to excite suspicion or even interest.

But the man was dead! There was no evidence whatever to show how he had come by his death, and the most convenient assumption was that he had died of "heart-stroke." The newspapers accordingly reported the sudden death of Johansson in the train as the result of heart disease, and the man's friends, and the public generally, accepted the newspaper statement without question.

The money which he should have had was not found on the body, but that did not for the moment excite comment, because so far as any one knew he might have paid it away before setting out on the journey, or possibly had not lifted it as had been stated.

In the meantime, however, the man's body was conveyed to his house, and a more careful examination brought to light the fact that death had been caused by blows on the head, from some heavy blunt instrument; that, in fact, there was no doubt whatever that he had been murdered.

Further inquiries elicited the fact that he had neither banked nor paid away the money he had with him, but carried bank notes to the value of several thousands of crowns on his person, or in a leathern case slung round his shoulders by a strap. This case was empty, and the fact of no money being found gave grounds for the inference that the unfortunate man had been murdered for the money which he carried.

Crimes of so violent a nature are so rare in Sweden, that the discovery caused great excitement and consternation throughout the country. As to who had done the deed there was no evidence whatever to show. No clue of any kind was found to guide the detectives in their search, and as day after day passed and no elucidation was forthcoming, people began to consider it a mystery that there was no hope of solving; when a strange rumour came from the town of Gefle which, in a sense, electrified all concerned in the inquiry, affording unlimited "copy" for the newspapers, as well as subjects for discussion and speculation to their readers.

The death of Johansson took place on the

18th of January, in the morning, and the rumour was that about the same hour of the same day a woman lying in her bed at Gefle —some three hundred or four hundred miles south of the scene of the murder—had a vision in which she saw the murder enacted, and which she related to her husband and others on awakening. The story of the vision I give here verbatim, as published in the local newspaper of Gefle, *Norlands-posten*, whence it was copied into almost every newspaper in the land.

Mrs. Holm, who is said to be connected with the Salvation Army, and is the wife of a respectable citizen of Gefle — a town on the north-east coast of Sweden — early on the morning of the 18th of January dreamed that she found herself somewhere north of Sundsvall, where Mr. Johansson resided. Of what she was doing there, or wanted to do, she had no clear idea, but she seemed to be bound for some place still further "upwards," that is to say, further north, and for this end in view she found herself at a railway station. There was no one else there. As she stood on the platform, waiting for the train, she noticed a large building in course of erection beside the station. The train drew up at the platform, and she stepped into a second-class carriage, and the train rushed on. The carriage in which she found herself was entered at the end, and divided into compartments, not after the style of the more elegant Pullman cars with a side corridor running the length of the carriage, but the compartments communicated with each other by doors in the middle of the walls which divided them, so that the guard or passengers could walk through the carriages from one end to the other, the seats on each side of the doors affording room for two persons.

The doors between the compartments had the upper panels of glass, so that any one sitting in one compartment, could, if so inclined, keep his eye on his neighbours next door.

She seated herself in one of the compartments. There were many people with the train, some of whom got out at the next station. She felt ashamed of being seen,

because she was ill-dressed and barefooted,
and when the train moved on, she got up from
her seat and walked through the carriage,
trying to find a compartment where she
might be alone. Passing into the one next to
where she had been sitting, she saw that it
was occupied by two men. One, the shortest
of them, was young, clean-shaven, blond,
and poorly clad, and had a heavy, sullen
face—evidently a peasant. The other was
a tall, well-built man, well dressed in fur-
lined pelisse, wore a "pincenez," had close-
cut whiskers and beard, and a dark moustache brushed upwards in the prevailing
fashion.

She smiled to herself, the contrast between
the friends being so great, the one so
fine a gentleman, and the other so simple
a peasant. Both looked at her in distinct
annoyance at her intrusion, and as it seemed
to her with a sort of watchfulness. She
passed therefore to the door of the next
compartment and looked through the glass.
It was the end compartment, and the back
seat was the full width of the carriage without a door to divide it. A man was lying

asleep on this seat. At first she thought it was her husband and wondered how he could have come there, but noticed immediately that the man's hair and beard were darker in colour, and that she had been mistaken.

She entered the compartment and, unnoticed by the sleeping man, seated herself in the corner farthest from him, hiding her naked feet under her skirts.

Immediately afterwards the door again opened, and a tall, broad-shouldered man entered. He was dressed in a winter cap and brownish overcoat, had round rather full cheeks, and full beard and moustache. Without taking the slightest notice of her, he took from his pocket a piece of lead, about two inches in length and tied in one corner of a red spotted handkerchief; glanced at the sleeper, who lay on his right side with his right arm under his head; and then dealt him a blow with the leaden weight just above the left ear.

The man seemed only to stretch himself a little. Behind him against the wall, she saw a leathern case or bag, but whether it lay loose, or was attached to his body by a strap, she could not see.

The murderer then tried to snatch the bag, but the partially-stunned man raised himself somewhat and grasped the bag with his left hand, whereupon the murderer dealt him another harder blow with the loaded kerchief, and his victim drew a deep breath, stretched himself out on the seat, and all was over.

The murderer, who was still seemingly unconscious of her presence, then opened the bag, and took from it several packets of bank notes, some large and square, others smaller and oblong. Taking a knife from his pocket, he opened his overcoat and made a slit in the lining, cutting from left to right. Then between the lining and the outer cloth he thrust the packets of notes, and laid the bag back into its place behind the dead man.

With a terrified scream Mrs. Holm awoke. It was then between four and five o'clock in the morning of January 18.

Her husband, aroused by her cry, inquired the cause of her alarm and she related the vision to him, at the same time expressing her conviction that their son, whom they were expecting home from a journey, had been murdered in the train. And it was only after being assured that her son could not possibly be in the part of the country of which she had dreamed, that she could be calmed. Although her nerves became gradually quietened, she stated her conviction that, if not her son, then some one else had been murdered in a train, and she eagerly scanned the newspapers to see if they held any verification of her dream.

It was not until four days later that the report of Johansson's death from heart-stroke in the train to Boden appeared in the newspaper. One of Mrs. Holm's sons was engaged in the printing office of the same paper, and after reading the notice she went to him, and asked if it was quite certain that Johansson had died a natural death. She spoke again of her vision, but her son assured her that had the man died from violence it would have been known, and he bade her not bother her head further about her dream.

Before the next issue of the newspaper,

however, news had come of the discovery
that Johansson had been murdered and
robbed. Together with these later particulars the newspaper printed the story of
the singular dream which, although known
some days earlier, had not been considered of
any value ; the editor even then simply com-
menting upon it as a curious coincidence.

The publication of this dream brought Mrs.
Holm into—for her—unenviable notoriety.
Interviewed by newspaper reporters, journa-
lists, detectives, and others, out of sheer
curiosity, she found herself in anything but
an agreeable position. Nothing new however was elicited, no further clue was found,
and so the matter, after being a nine days'
wonder, gradually ceased to be of absorbing
interest ; and the discovery of the murderer
of the ill-fated Johansson was apparently no
nearer.

.   .   .   .   .

At different times during the previous two
or three years, several robberies had taken
place in different parts of the north of
Sweden. Despite their utmost efforts, the
police had not been able to discover the

guilty parties, or to bring a charge against any single person, although they were morally convinced that a man called Westermark-Rosén was concerned in most of them, either alone or in conjunction with a gang of thieves, of which it was suspected he was the leader.

But with all their skill the detectives failed to discover any proof against him. Several times he had been charged with certain crimes, but in all cases an *alibi* was proven, and the man—sorely against the inclination of the magistrates—was perforce released triumphant and insolent, vowing revenge on his detractors and accusers.

This Westermark-Rosén was said to be a well-educated, accomplished man, but a thorough scoundrel, cunning and wily as a fox, and a good actor; able to assume at will the character most suited to the design he wished to carry out. All this was known to the emissaries of the law, yet he, knowing the law as well as the best of them, contrived to baffle them completely. They could never catch him red handed, and, although at times the evidence was so strong that his conviction seemed certain, yet there

was always a sufficient proof that he, at
the time of the perpetration of the crime,
was engaged in some very ordinary business
a hundred miles away, there being no lack
of people to testify to the fact.

It was generally supposed that the man
had a "double," and that they worked to
each other's hands, the "double" being very
much in evidence in some particular place,
while Westermark-Rosén, in another character, committed the depredation.

However he managed, he did it cleverly;
but the cleverest can at some time over-
reach himself, and so it happened that he
was taken before the magistrates charged
with some lesser theft from which he failed
to free himself. During the inquiry the
detectives, ever on the alert in regard to
the murder of Johansson, tried to prove that
the accused man had been in the neighbourhood, if not on the train, when the
murder took place; but the usual *alibi*
was pleaded, and several persons were called
who swore that he was in another part of
Sweden at the time.

The inquiry created much discussion, and

the public demanded that Westermark-Rosén should be kept in confinement till the murderer had been discovered, the impression of his guilt being stronger than the evidence of his innocence. Several months had elapsed since the murder of Johansson, when it was decided to bring Mrs. Holm to the court, and, unknown to her, into the presence of Westermark-Rosén and his accomplice in the theft with which he stood charged.

Such is briefly the story of Westermark-Rosén, and his position at the time. I now resume the story as told by the newspapers.

Mrs. Holm was conducted north to the court to give her evidence respecting her remarkable dream. When on the railway, the train stopped at the station of Bastutrask —the station before Jörn ; and looking out of the carriage window, she cried—

"It was here that in my dream I got into the train, but the house they were then building, where is it ? "

"There is the house they were erecting at the time," replied Herr Styrlander, who was escorting her (pointing to a large building near the station), "but it was finished and ready some time ago."

The railway carriage she could not re-cognise. The interior arrangements, she said, were quite different. Yet she was travelling then in the very same carriage in which the murder was committed. This she could not understand. The guard was called and questioned, and he stated that after the murder the carriage had been altered and entirely refitted, the old doorways and di-viding walls being removed, and a corridor running the length of one side of the carri-age being made instead. At the time of the murder it was just as Mrs. Holm described as having seen it in her dream.

On Tuesday morning, immediately before the opening of the court, Mrs. Holm, ac-companied by another lady, was brought into the anteroom of the hall of justice. There were a number of persons waiting to be called, and several in attendance to watch the result. Walking round the room with an officer of the court, Mrs. Holm stopped suddenly near two men who were quietly

P

seated. The one had an overcoat lying across his knees, the lining turned outwards.

"Here must be the murderer's coat," she exclaimed.

The man started up with an oath, letting fall the coat. Looking him full in the face, she added, "And this is the man I saw murder Johansson in the train."

It was Westermark-Rosén, who was handcuffed, and the man beside him was a prison warder.

Later, when being questioned in the court, the judge asked, "Do you recognise in the prisoner, Westermark-Rosén, the person you dreamed you saw murder Johansson?" She answered unhesitatingly, "Yes."

"Do you recognise the overcoat he wore?"

To this she also replied without hesitation, "Yes, I feel sure, if you examine it, it will be found to have a slit in the lining at the right-hand side where he hid the bank-notes."

Thereupon the coat was carefully examined, and in the lining, on the side indicated by the witness, was found a neatly sewn seam that had once been a cut across, and had been carefully repaired.

Westermark - Rosén had turned deadly
pale, and for the first time during this long
inquiry seemed to lose control over himself.
He was greatly agitated, his eyes wandering
searchingly about him, as if looking for
some means of escape. He carefully avoided
looking at Mrs. Holm, although ordered to
do so. It was fully fifteen minutes before
he recovered his usual cool, somewhat insolent deportment. When he spoke it was
with an evident effort, but he remarked non-
chalantly, "There is nothing remarkable in
such a dream; in these enlightened times
such things can be explained."

In the meantime the man Viklund, Westermark-Rosén's accomplice in the robbery for
which they were being tried, was quietly
brought into court, and placed where Mrs.
Holm could not fail to see him. Her attention was in nowise drawn to him, but
the moment her glance fell on him she
seemed to recognise him, and then, pointing
to him, said, "That is the young man who
sat in the compartment next to where
Johansson was murdered."

Viklund replied to this only by a broad grin.

W. Rosén, who usually talked to, questioned, scoffed, sneered at, and cross-questioned the witnesses, in order to bewilder and make them contradict themselves, and who only that day had been removed from the court in consequence of this unseemly behaviour, was, during the examination of Mrs. Holm, absolutely silent, and nervously ill at ease.

The result of Mrs. Holm's evidence caused a profound sensation, which was not lessened by the nervousness displayed by the prisoner; but although judge, jury, and, in fact, all in the crowded court, as well as the general public, expressed their undoubted conviction that Westermark-Rosén was guilty of the murder of Johansson, still the law does not take dreams into account as legal evidence, and therefore he could only be sentenced for some other lesser crimes for which he stood arraigned.

The judge, in summing up the case, said he regretted he could " do no more than this."

A sentence of three years' imprisonment was passed, which was the extreme limit of the law for such offences as were proved against him.

This sentence was looked upon by the general public as a sort of remand to give time for further developments, but up to the present no more light has been thrown on the matter.

Westermark-Rosén has since been released from prison, and the murder as well as the dream bid fair to remain what they have been up to the present—a mystery.

.   .   .   .   .   .

I will now very briefly relate my own experience of excursions taken in the dream state. Once, when staying at Mr. Sjöstedt's in Christiania, I was, as I thought, awakened by the clanging of bells. I was very tired and wanted to sleep, but could not do so. It appeared to me that I got up and went out to see why they were making such a terrible noise. How I passed from my room I do not know, but once outside I felt that the slightest touch of the ground was sufficient to carry me several hundred feet; so I amused myself in practising this method of flying. Just then it seemed that Mr. S. joined me, and I taught him how to fly. I then went to the church, returned to my room, and went to sleep. In the morning, when at breakfast, Mr. S. said, "I had a very curious dream. I thought I was out with you, and that you taught me to fly." We then discussed our various dreams and found that they coincided; so I went over to the church to see how far the rest of the dream might be true. I found the church in every respect the same inside as that which I had visited. I saw the belfry and the ringers; and the old man—the caretaker—I particularly recognised as he was dusting the seats.

Some time after this I was visiting some friends in Berlin, and on the Saturday night, after I had retired, I dreamed I was out in the streets, that it was raining, and that I had little more on than my night dress. Not knowing the city, I was afraid I might not find my way home. Just then a woman rushed out of an opening and fled past me, screaming "Murder! Police!" She was closely followed by a man, with a knife in his hand, who, I seemed to know, was following her to prevent her giving information of a murder of another woman which he

had just then committed. I felt frightened
and hurried home, and, having awakened
between one and two in the morning, I felt
so certain that I had been out and experienced what I have described, that I got up to
examine my dress and shoes, and to look for
the wet splashes of rain, but all bore evidence
of the fact that I had not left my room since
retiring a few hours previously. Next day,
being Sunday, I heard of nothing to corrobo-
rate my dream, but on the Monday when the
morning papers came there was a full report
of the murder.

After this I tried various experiments in
order to further explain what I have related.
I wrote to a friend saying, " I tried to visit
you last night and it seems to me I succeeded,
but all is not clear; there is a vague impression of something particular as to some
flowers." My friend replied, " I was sitting
writing until one o'clock in the morning, and
alongside of me was a little rose tree with
two roses in bloom. Just before retiring, I
lifted it from the table and put it in its place
on the flower stand. In the morning, about
seven, I found the roses were cut off and

lying beside the stem on the top of the mould."

Sometime after this, when in Helsingfors, the foregoing incidents were discussed, and I was asked if I would try an experiment whereby my friends there might be satisfied of the possibility of what I had related.

"It would be very interesting. For instance, now that you are going to Petersburg, could you not try to pay us a visit from there?"

"I do not know," I replied dubiously; "I don't think trying has much to do with it. On those occasions I was asleep and helpless, so far as the exercise of my will was concerned."

"But you can try," urged my hostess. "One does not know one's powers till one tries. If it has been done once involuntarily you may succeed again. Anyway, promise to try."

"I can promise so much," I said, "but I feel sure it is of no use. I don't even know how to go about it. I can only think hard."

"Well, 'think hard' on Wednesday night, and we will be here waiting for you in this room. We will sit here from ten to eleven o'clock and think about you coming. If we cannot see you, you can perhaps make some little sign that we may know you are here; for instance, move the candlestick which will be on the table; or if you cannot do that, rattle the glass collar on the top of it which we will be sure to hear."

I agreed to make the attempt, but remarked that it was possible I should not be able to dispose of my time, as I did not know what programme my friends in Petersburg might have arranged for me.

"True," they said; "then we will say either Wednesday or Thursday night, between ten and eleven. We will be here both evenings; that will give you a better chance."

Next day found me in St. Petersburg, and I confess I forgot all about my arrangement till, on retiring to bed on the Wednesday night, I heard the clock strike twelve. I felt rather guilty, but consoled myself with the reflection that the whole evening had been taken up with visitors, so that even had I remembered, it would have been impossible to be alone without exciting remark.

The next evening I went to my room earlier. It was a few minutes after ten. I stood before my toilette table, perplexed and wondering what I should do. I was not sleepy, nor likely to fall asleep immediately, even if I hurried over my hair-brushing and undressing operations. The time too was slipping away. I wondered how much the time varied between Petersburg and Helsingfors, if it were earlier or later there, but I could not reckon it out. In fact, I could not, somehow, keep hold of my thoughts; they would go flying about first here, then there, and I was beginning to feel a little flurried and anxious.

Pulling myself together as it were, I said to my reflection in the mirror before me, "'This won't do, you've made a promise and you've got to keep it if you can. You had better set yourself to work to think hard, as you arranged; and remember those good people in Helsingfors are depending on the performance of your part of the agreement."

Thus admonished I turned from the glass and sat down before the writing-table, on which a green-shaded reading lamp was burning, and placing my elbows on the table, and my face in my hands, I wondered how I was to begin.

"I will imagine I am going there," I said to myself. So I began in my fancy to leave my room and pass down the stairs into the street, then along to the Finnish Railway, and by train to Helsingfors. On my arrival there I walked through the hard-frozen, snow-covered streets, noting a few passers-by, the houses, the church, the lighted lamps, and thought to myself, " how dismal and still the town is at this hour of night." I entered the boulevard where my friends' house was situated, noting the snow-covered trees and bushes in the park. Then it struck me that it was after ten o'clock, and the entrance gates would be locked, so that I could not get into the house. I reached the gates, they were unfastened, and as I pushed them open I smiled to myself and thought, " What a funny idea it is, I to be sitting here staring at a green lamp shade, yet imagining a journey and taking notes of my imaginary peregrinations as if they were actually taking place." But even these reflections made me to some extent loose hold, as it were, on my intention to follow out the fancied journey, and I resolutely shut my eyes to the lamp shade and other surroundings, forcing myself in thought to ascend the many stairs leading to the various *étages*. I even counted the steps as I ascended—a habit I have had since childhood when going up or down stairs. As I reached the third *étage*, the recollection of a pair of galoshes I had once seen standing there, like the feet of a sentinel who had been spirited away leaving his foot gear behind him, made me laugh as I had laughed at the time.

I passed on up the other flights of stairs and placed my hand on the door handle. It turned and I went in, making my way through the *entreé* into the drawing-room, which was in darkness. I knew the arrangement of the furniture, and by its means groped my way to the door of the room I had occupied, and where it was decided I should come. I turned the door handle softly and looked in—surprised to note the room was in utter darkness. I was a little startled at my feeling of surprise, which brought me again back to the consciousness of sitting at the writing-

table in a house on Newski Prospect, Petersburg, but with an effort I put this to one
side, for I felt a growing interest in my
fancied excursion, and was afraid of losing
any part of the impressions that were so
real to me.

I stood looking into the dark room,
wondering why it was dark, and why I could
not have imagined it lighted up instead, and
whether any one were in the room.

As I stood peering into the darkness I
began to be conscious that there were
persons in the room, and also to note that
a faint light on one side indicated where
the windows were. By degrees I could
distinguish some dark shapes or shadows
dimly defined against the white walls of
the room. I counted these shadows; there
were ten. I knew they must be persons,
but I had not expected to find more than
six—the members of the family. I could
not recognize any of them; it was too
dark. Turning towards the window, I saw
another shadow, more clearly outlined against
the faintly lighted white curtains, and something in its shape made me think of Captain

T.   I watched it curiously for a moment
and thought, "If it is the captain he will
have on his uniform."   I moved over to
where the form sat against the window
curtain, and put out my hand to touch the
shoulder and sleeve of his coat.   It was
not a uniform, therefore I decided that the
form was not that of the captain.

Standing now with my back to what
little light there was, it seemed to me that
I could distinguish the different contours
of the other figures, and I said to myself,
"If I had not been mistaken in respect to
the captain, I should have said the figure
to the right was that of General T., and
the one a little to the left his wife; but
it's all nonsense, any way.   I am not really
seeing anything, I am sitting in my dressing-
gown by a table, my hair hanging loose
over my shoulders, fabricating a dream.   I
had much better go to bed."

Even while admonishing myself, I seemed
to be standing beside the figure I had
thought to be the captain, when suddenly
I saw another shadow or figure I had not
previously noticed, crouched on the floor

between the sofa and the supposed captain.
I wondered a little at this, and wondered,
too, at my own invention of surprises, but
all the same I decided that the crouching
figure must be Ebba, the youngest of the
family, as I remembered her habit of sitting
on a low stool or on the carpet if interested in any conversation that might be
going on; and I smiled to myself at the
freaks fancy could play, bringing out little
forgotten circumstances as though they were
being re-acted before one's eyes.

I had a feeling that there was something
I ought to do or say, and I puzzled myself
in vain to think what it was. I glanced
round the darkened room for a clue that
might suggest to my mind what this forgotten something could be; but I gave it
up—I could not remember.

Something, a sound of a door opening,
or a bell ringing, startled me, and my
imaginings vanished.

I felt a little amused at my attempt to
"think hard," but at the same time dis-
satisfied with myself, thinking that if I had
gone to bed and had fallen asleep it was

possible the imaginings might have taken a more tangible form; but now it was past eleven o'clock and I was feeling curiously weak and tired.

A few days later I returned to Helsingfors.

"You did not come on Wednesday night," remarked my friends, as we sat at dinner that first evening.

"No, I was unable to leave the company till too late," I replied, thinking to myself that I would not confess I had forgotten. "Were you there waiting?"

"Yes, we were all there, and on Thursday also—did you not try?"

"Yes; I tried, but, you see, I did not in the least know how to go about it, and then I did not get to my room till ten o'clock, and so could not get to sleep in time, so had no hope of succeeding. I did try to fix my thoughts on you all, and tried to imagine I was in the room and saw you all sitting there; but of course I knew it was all imagination, for I really do not think one can do anything like that of one's own will, although I could imagine I saw you all sitting so solemnly in the darkness waiting."

" Yes, we thought you could manage better if we had no light burning."

" Oh! that was curious. Do you know, when I tried to fancy myself here, I was a little surprised to find the room quite dark, and it seemed to me that there were ten of you—no, eleven," I corrected as I remembered the crouching figure I had not seen when I had counted the shadowy forms.

"There were only ten of us."

I began to feel a little creepy sensation tingling to my finger-tips.

" Did the captain sit near the far window with his back to it?"

" Yes."

" And the general to the right of the table near the stove?"

" Yes."

" And Mrs. T. at his left?"

" Yes."

" And three persons on the sofa opposite the door?"

" Yes."

We looked at each other in growing astonishment.

" The captain did not wear his uniform?"

Q

" Yes, he did."

" Then it's all nonsense; the other things are only coincidences, for if I were really here, the figure I took to be the captain did not wear a uniform. And Ebba—did she not sit on the floor or a low stool between the sofa and the captain ? "

" No ! " said Ebba, " I sat on the sofa between my sister and Miss H."

" Mistake number two ! I fancied some one sat like that, and naturally thought of Ebba."

" No one sat like that."

So the subject was dismissed and the conversation drifted into other channels. Later, when the captain joined us, he broached the matter again, and I related my attempt to think myself into their midst, mentioning the small discrepancies and coincidences, the uniform, Ebba's position, &c.

" But I did not wear my uniform," exclaimed the captain ; " I was wet with snow and changed for a house jacket when I came in. I sat near the window with my back to it and not near any one else. While sitting there, I distinctly felt a hand touch

my shoulder. You remember I said so,"
turning to the others. "It quite startled
me ; it touched me first on the shoulder and
stroked downwards to my wrist."

I had not said a word about my imagined
examination of the captain's coat sleeve.

"Yes!" exclaimed the others. "We
remember your saying some one was touching you."

"It was to be heard plainly enough,"
rejoined the captain. "I told B., who was
sitting nearest, to listen and he would hear
the rustle, so he came and knelt down beside
me to hear if it came a second time."

"Then it was Barrister B. who was
crouching on the floor, whom you mistook
for Ebba!"

The matter was beginning to assume a
new aspect, and I had a strange, startled
feeling, that was not altogether pleasant.

"Then why didn't you touch the candlestick?"

Now I remembered what had puzzled me,
what I had forgotten and tried to recall, as
I stood hesitating and wondering in the
dark room.

"I had forgotten. I tried to remember, and looked for something that might recall what I had to do, but it was so dark. I do not think I even saw a candlestick; if I had I'm sure I should have recollected."

"We should have left it standing on the table," remarked Countess W.; "then you would have seen it, but some one said that if the table moved it might be thrown down and broken. So we put it in the niche of the stove. It could not easily be seen there in the darkness, but that we did not think about."

Now curiously enough the chain was complete, and my notes of my imaginary visit confirmed—

1st. The room was in darkness.

2nd. There were ten persons in the room.

3rd. Three of them sat in the positions I had seen—viz., the general, his wife, and the captain.

4th. The captain did not wear his uniform.

5th. My touch on his coat sleeve had been heard, felt, and commented on.

6th. The crouching figure was a fact, and my mistake as to there being eleven persons in the room was accounted for by the fact of the barrister changing his place unnoticed by me.

7th. The incident of the candlestick being removed from the table was a sufficient reason for my non-recollection of the action I had agreed upon.

Now the question arises: "Is it possible that all these things were mere coincidences?" If any one were to ask me, I should say unhesitatingly "No!"

At the same time I do not attempt to put forward any theory to explain them, though I firmly believe that we mortals are endowed with unsuspected and un-understood powers, which, if studied and cultivated, would open up a vast field for research.

THE LIGHT OF PENTRAGINNY

THIS story was told to me many years ago, when spending a school holiday on the south-west coast of England.

Captain Hanna, a naval officer, was then the captain of the coast-guard. One fine day his daughters and myself went with him out to sea to inspect some buoys. "Father, tell us about the angel buoy at Pentraginny," said one of the girls, and turning to me, she added, "You must hear it; it's the strangest story you can imagine. Every one knows about it, and father was born near the place and knew all the people quite well—not Marah, because she was dead before he was born, but all the others in the village he knew."

That evening Captain Hanna told us the story. I do not know the dates, but it is thirty years since that summer evening, and the captain was then somewhere about sixty years old, so that places the time back nearly a century.

Pentraginny is one of a hundred small hamlets scattered on the rock-bound coast of Cornwall, inhabited solely by fishermen and their families. It contains only a score or two of houses, mostly low whitewashed cottages, with thatched roofs, and adjacent sheds for drying, salting, or smoking of fish. Each cottage possesses a patch of ground where the women cultivate potatoes. These patches are surrounded by fences which serve the double purpose of keeping out the pigs and forming a convenient drying place for the fishing nets, which are usually to be seen festooned around them.

Some of the more affluent of the families possess a cow or two, but with one or two exceptions they were at that time, though happily content, all alike dependent on the sea for their subsistence; these exceptions being the keeper of the little inn and Captain Daniels, the most important man in Pentraginny and the fortunate owner of some three or four staunch, well-fitted fishing smacks,

as well as of the brig *Martha*, which
latter he had inherited from his wife's father.
David Daniels had served as man and boy
on board the *Martha*, and finally, when
he had taken his "captain's ticket," had
married its owner's only daughter, whose
namesake it was. Captain Daniels was,
therefore, an important man, whose opinions
carried more weight than those of any one
else in Pentraginny, and to whom in fact
the parish clergyman paid great deference.

The hamlet boasted an inn, where it was
usual for the male population to meet of an
evening to discuss the arrangements for the
next season's harvest, namely, the pilchard
fishing, and the prospects of the same, news
of the signs preceding the coming of the
small fish being eagerly sought for and commented upon. The fortunes of the Pentraginny men, as well as those of hundreds
of other villages, turned upon the results of
this particular fishery, so that it naturally was
an absorbing topic of conversation, that and the
family affairs of the community, for, as in many
such small settlements, the inhabitants were all
more or less distantly related one to another.

There existed a strictly conservative spirit amongst them, which caused a marriage of the young people with "foreigners"—that is to say, persons from another district—to be looked upon with distinct disfavour. When, therefore, Naomi, the daughter of old Simeon, the elder brother of "Captain Daniels," married a young Welshman who built a cottage and settled down near the old people, he was regarded as an intruder, against whom, as well as against any possible encroachments on their rights on his part, they were prepared to act on the defensive.

However, the necessity for this social boycotting was soon removed, for within a year of the marriage the brave young Welshman lost his life in trying to save that of others from a vessel that was driven on to, and impaled upon, the sunken rocks which guard the little bay.

Within a few hours of the catastrophe, Naomi died in giving birth to the babe whom with her latest breath she called "Marah," the child of bitterness and sorrow.

The child thus orphaned at its birth was a tacit reproach to the rough fisher-folk for

their treatment of her parents, and they
seemed to regard it as their duty to make
amends by kindness to her for their want of
it to the young couple, who were buried in
one grave immediately after the baptism of
their little daughter.

"She should have been named 'Angela,'
not 'Marah,'" the parson had been heard to
remark once when the infant had grown into
a small maiden of five or six summers, for
she was not like other children : so pale,
so fair, so sweet ; her large innocent eyes
seemed to look out into the world with a
quaint serious gravity that sat oddly on the
baby face.

No ! She was not like the other children ;
the serious, wistful baby face had not the
look of the ruddy, apple-cheeked bairns of
the fisher-folk. She looked "like a spirit
from another world," the people would say,
and the hearts of her grandparents would
seem to stand still with fear, when they
would sometimes see their darling at the
open doorway surrounded by a halo of
golden sunshine. There was so little of
earth in the child's delicate face and slender

figure, that it seemed to them she would
suddenly spread some unsuspected wings,
rise up into the sunshine, and disappear from
their sight.

The loss of their children had affected
the old couple sorely, and on the child
Marah, they lavished all the love of their
bereaved hearts, old Simeon asking nothing
better than to follow her baby footsteps
whither they led him, never checking their
course unless to avoid a danger, patiently
waiting when the child sat in her favourite
haunt on a boulder of rock looking seaward, looking out towards the distant horizon
with a rapt earnest gaze as though studying
some great mystery.

"What do you see, my babe?" old Simeon
would sometimes say, in a tremor of a vague,
undefined fear, when he would see an unconscious smile play over the child's features,
and notice the eagerness of her eyes.

"They are speaking to me from the water.
Listen! Can you not hear them?" she had
replied once; and afterwards, when he noticed
her eager listening attitude, the old man
would fearfully gather the child in his arms

and totter homewards, feeling as though some mysterious power was dragging the little one from him, and the only safety for him and for her was far away from the alluring voice of the waves.

Next to sitting dreaming by the sea, she loved best to sit at the old man's side in the porch, and listen while he talked of Naomi and her brave young husband, of the terrible day of the storm, when he risked his life and lost it, and how she, Naomi, could not live without him, so had gone with him to heaven, leaving little Marah to comfort the old people for their loss.

"So they left us for ever," the old man would conclude; "our two blessed children. They are happy in another world, where there are no more storms, nor death, nor parting. Perhaps we may meet them again—God knows. His ways are wonderful ways, and an old man cannot understand them. The parson says we will meet again sometime, but it's a long time to wait, and who knows but in that beautiful place where God lives, they'll be so happy together, praising and singing and playing on their golden harps, they'll never have time to think of us; and we'll be getting older and older, they'll not know us again when we go to them."

The old man's head would drop regretfully on his breast, and a tear would steal down his furrowed cheek, as his fingers lingered on the soft fair hair of the child, who would listen with a far-away look in the blue eyes to the old man's words.

"She doesn't forget, grandfer; she comes so often when you and grandmother are sleeping, and she says to me, 'Be good and kind to him, Marah; and be a loving child to her.' And I know she means you and grandmother, for she goes to your bed-side and looks down at you, and smiles. Then she comes back to me, and puts her cheek on mine, and puts her arm around me, but you and grandmother never know, for you sleep so soundly. Sometimes a man comes with her, and she says it is Nathaniel, my father, and he kisses me; then they go away. So, you see, they don't forget us; you need not be afraid."

The heart of the old man misgave him sorely when the child would try to comfort him by such strange words. It was not natural nor childlike, and though it was sweet to think that their lost Naomi watched over her little one in the darkness of the night, it filled the old people with a vague terror to hear the child speak of her dreams as though they were so real and palpable to her.

So the time passed, and when at length the dreamy gentle child had grown into a dreamy gentle maiden of fifteen years, old Simeon and Ruth laid down the burden of life, and were taken to rest beside their children in the churchyard.

Marah became the inmate of the queer little brown house on the hill, and the adopted daughter of Captain and Mistress Daniels. Their family had hitherto consisted of one girl, Gennifer; but, as the neighbours were wont to remark, Gennifer was equal to half-a-dozen. She was the prettiest girl for miles around. Strong, lithe, supple of limb, she could climb the rocks or row a boat as skilfully as any of the youths who admired and secretly adored the bright, merry, hoydenish lass.

Gennifer professed an unbounded contempt for the slender proportions and timid nature of the younger girl, but a genuine affection existed between them nevertheless. It was often said that Marah was like an angel in the house, and both Gennifer and her parents were always ready to endorse that opinion.

The Scar is a low ridge of outlying rocks, running parallel with the shore, nearly closing the entrance to the little bay. These sunken rocks act as a breakwater on which the great waves, rolling in from the Atlantic, break their force, leaving the snug little harbour within undisturbed by their fury. Here in the worst weather the fleet of fishing smacks ride safely at their anchors, or lie moored to the jetty running out from the shore.

In the old wrecking days, many a fair barque met her fate on the needle-like rocks of the Scar, lured thereto by the wreckers' fires. Even now in storms, the experienced seaman running for shelter avoids the Scar with horror, although the smooth water within presents a haven of peace and safety —if he could only reach it; but the risk of making the narrow channel between the sunken rocks is too great, unless, indeed, the barque is guided by the hand of one familiar with them, and knows every point, every shallow, every opening between them, as do the fisher-folk of the village.

At low water the submerged rocks are barely covered; indeed some of the higher points always show themselves as the waves recede, but during flood and spring tides there is nothing to show the treachery lurking under the surface. For small craft there is little or no danger at such times, there being sufficient water at flood tide to carry the largest fishing smack safely over the needle-like ridges and points; and no other vessel ever came into the bay by design, except the brig *Martha* whose commander knew every tooth of the Scar as well as he knew every tooth in his head.

Ships had been known to drive on those rocks, when by stress of weather they had been induced to seek shelter in the nearest harbour; but of late years no casualties had happened — not since the time when young Nathaniel had lost his life in trying to save those of the shipwrecked crew.

Since then a lighthouse had been built, some three miles to the west of the village, and its bright revolving light flashed a constant warning to all passing vessels of the danger to be avoided. So the Scar, instead of being an enemy to be feared, was a friend to be thankful for, guarding as it did the little bay from the fury of storm and sea.

At low water there is but one opening where a vessel may safely pass, and this is so well known that no one had ever deemed it necessary to mark the spot by a light. Certainly a buoy was there, on which a little red flag fluttered its signal to the home - returning fishers, but on dark nights this was not much of a guide.

Sometimes, indeed, when any anxiety was felt for an absent smack, the question was raised as to whether there ought not to be a light placed near it; but sailors and fishers are proverbially a careless race, and the question was never answered by the placing of a light there.

R

When the fleet was known to be in the offing, and likely to be making for home at dark, the young people would sometimes row out to the Scar and burn packets of Bengal fire, as a signal and welcome to the returning boats. This practice was regarded by the old sailors in the light of an amusement and waste of money, rather than as a necessary precaution. In fact, the more sober-minded set their faces against such pyrotechnic displays, as they were generally the forerunners of other extravagances in the same direction, frequently finishing up by the gathering together of all the young people to dance and otherwise enjoy themselves at the village inn, till the stroke of midnight and closing time brought the festivities to an end.

It had been a rough, boisterous day, following a succession of several more or less stormy ones. From early morning the wind had veered round from all quarters, but in the afternoon it had blown steadily from the south-west, and as evening approached it settled earnestly to its work of lashing the sea into a perfect fury. The western sky at sunset was aflame with fiery clouds, brilliant and beautiful to look upon, but to the fisher-folk gazing seaward fraught with ominous meaning.

"A nasty sundown!" they remarked to each other as they made their boats more secure at their moorings, and took in and stowed away the flapping sails, or any loose cordage lying about.

"It'll be a wild night, an' them as is outside'll have plenty ter do."

Fortunately all the fishers were safely at home; none of them were exposed to the increasing storm, so they could converse comfortably as they blew the clouds of tobacco smoke from them, and speculated on the probable duration of the gale that gathered in violence as the sun sank lower.

"Dost remember the storm when young Nat was drowned? 'Twas just such another. Aa mind how the sun set in a flame like as ter night."

"Ay! Aa mind et well; 'twas a sad time for the old folk ter lose 'em both in the same day. Sad, too, for the little maid.   Seems ter me, neighbour, 'at the maid Marah's never been like other maids, allus for hersel' like, as ef her dedn't belong ter same folk."

"'Twas the shock ter Naomi as ded et; the maid es a bet fey."

"Fey! Nay, Aa wouldn't call her 'fey'; her es allus too quiet an' still-like for thet, but her seems ter hev a unnerstannin' o' things 'at's sort o' onnatteral. When her was a little maid 'twas more noticeable 'an 'tis now."

Just then a brilliant flash shot out over the stormy sea, and the speakers gazed with pride and interest at the warning gleam sent forth from the noble lighthouse a few miles to the west of them. The existence of the beacon gave them a sense of security they had not known in their younger days.   There had been exciting episodes in the lives of these old weather-beaten fishers before the erection of the lighthouse, and these, with the shipwrecks on the Scar, formed the theme of many a long story told in the village inn.   The younger generation knew them all by heart, and, it may be, privately questioned the veracity of the story-tellers, for nothing so interesting ever happened nowadays.

All knew of the disaster which had orphaned the delicate fragile Marah, but that was so long ago—sixteen years—and, it may be, the hearts of the village youth would not have been sad had a spice of some similar adventures been sprinkled in their own lives.

On this day of the storm, most of the young people were away in the neighbouring village celebrating a wedding. Gennifer Daniels had been bridesmaid-in-chief, and prime promoter of the fun and amusement among the many guests. Her father, accompanied by her adopted sister, Marah, had joined the guests later in the day. Captain Daniels had tried to excuse himself, but Gennifer would not hear of it. Marah, shy and timid, wished to remain at home, but Mrs. Daniels, declaring herself better than she had felt for many a day, insisted on the girl donning the pretty white gown, and betaking herself to the wedding party. As evening closed in, the fun began in earnest. Gennifer was in her element, the life and soul of the party, but Captain Daniels, in spite of his pleasure in the society of young people and his pride in his daughter, had appeared restless and ill at ease all the afternoon, and Marah noticed that he took an early opportunity to slip away from the company.

He had wandered to a bit of rising ground near to the house of merry-making, and stood gazing seaward, not that he could see the ocean, but he scanned the western sky with an anxious look. The red glow had not yet quite faded, and the moon was rising, though for the most part obscured by heavy broken clouds.

"It'll be a nasty night or I'm much mistaken," he said to himself. "Pity the brig did not get in before the change came! I've a mind to take a run down an' see how it looks outside." He buttoned his jacket over his broad chest, and pulled his soft felt hat more firmly on his head, as he turned with the intention of making his way down to the sea, when a white-clad, slender figure came to his side.

"Where are you going, father?" asked Marah, and she held his arm tightly to steady herself against a violent gust of wind.

"No ways in particular, my maid. I thought I'd like to see how it looks outside, but go thy ways, and dance wi' rest of 'em!"

"I don't want to dance, father, I'd rather go home; we've been away from mother so long. I feel I must go, and they'll never miss me up yonder."

"You're a queer maid to run away from fun an' dancin', but if you're set on it, I'll see you a bit on the way. Tie the shawl well over you and hold on to me, or the wind will carry you away."

With quick steps they made their way homewards, the gathering darkness and the violent gusts of wind making it no easy matter, though the moon gleamed out fitfully from between the heavy clouds that scudded over her surface.

When they reached a point from which the sea was visible, Captain Daniels stopped, and gazed earnestly out over the white-crested waves, while Marah sheltered herself behind his broad shoulders.

"Did'st see ought, Marah?" he asked, as the moon was once more darkened and they resumed their way.

"No, father; did you think you saw something?"

"Nay! I'm not sure, but I'm uneasy for the brig; she ought to have been here by now."

"Captain Evans knows the coast, father; and he is careful."

"Yes, for sure!"

They had gone but a few steps further when they were met by a man from Pentraginny.

"Is't Cap'n Daniels?" he inquired, peering through the darkness. "Aa thought aa'd come an' warn you 'at the brig's outside, an' looks as if her was makin' for ter come in wi' tide."

"I wasn't mistaken then," said the captain, "when I thought I saw something."

The three hurried on as quickly as the wind permitted, exchanging a word now and again to express a wish that the brig was safely within the Scar, or that the moon might prove a friend, and remain unobscured during the coming in.

"I wish Evans would lie off till daylight," said Captain Daniels uneasily. "It's not like him to attempt to run in with a sea like this."

But there could be no doubt as to Captain Evans' intention; the brig was heading for the harbour, the tide was near the flood, and the wind, though blowing a hurricane, was a fair one. Captain Evans knew every point of the Scar as he knew his own fingers; yet the attempt seemed to the watchers on shore to be little short of madness.

Captain Daniels watched with the rest, without responding to the frequent remarks of the fishermen, who stood in groups on the sands, watching the swiftly approaching vessel. In less than half-an-hour the tide would be at the full, and it was evident that Captain Evans had timed it so that the vessel should ride over the Scar at the flood.

Marah walked by the captain's side, and though he was silent, she knew by the intermittent clouds of smoke from the frequently replenished pipe, that he was nervously anxious. But she did not know all that was troubling him, nor of the neglect to renew the insurance of the ship and her cargo. It was this thought which held the captain tongue-tied as he watched, with beating heart and straining eyes, the rapidly nearing vessel.

The fishers watched eagerly. In spite of the gale the brig seemed to make no account of the difficulties, but rode steadily on, guided by a masterly hand; and notwithstanding his anxiety, Captain Daniels felt a thrill of pride in seeing his bonny *Martha* behaving so well.

The moon disappeared behind a heavy bank of cloud, from which there was no hope of her emerging for some time, and the darkness became intense.

"Red fire!" Who was it suggested it? Yes! that was a good idea.

In an incredibly short time the Bengal lights were at hand, and three or four men, including the captain, had jumped into a boat and were pushing off, when Marah with a spring placed herself at his side, with—

"Let me come too, father!"

Captain Daniels grumbled, but there was no time to lose, and the men bent to their oars. Arrived at the Scar they laboured to keep the boat "mid channel" whilst Captain Daniels, with Marah's help, lit and held aloft the blazing torches that shed a brilliant glow over the faces of the men in the boat.

Over and over again the fire flamed out, and in the intervals of darkness the men strained their eyes to see what progress the brig had made, but dazzled by the red glare they could discern nothing. Lying in the trough of the sea, struggling to keep the little boat "end on," they could not always see the lights of the vessel for the waves which rose up on every side, till one larger than the rest lifted the little boat on its crest; then they saw the brig, but it was a sight that struck terror to the hearts of the men, and almost paralysed their arms, so great was their consternation to see that the brig had altered her course, and was making straight for the most dangerous points of the Scar.

No words were needed to express their horror. No cries, no voice, could reach the fated vessel; the wind blew back the sounds; they could only watch and wait for the awful moment; they could *do* nothing.

After the first terrified cry from the rowers, they had not uttered a word. They mechanically kept the boat in position, and Captain Daniels lit another torch and held it above their heads.

In the brilliant glare they saw what they had not noticed earlier, that the girl Marah had fainted and lay as if dead, her eyes closed, and her hair drenched with the waves that from time to time broke over them.

They said nothing—a girl's fainting fit was not of much account in the face of this impending disaster.

The moments seemed like hours, as they waited for the sound of the grinding of the *Martha's* keel on the Needles. Again the Bengal torches were lighted, but did not help them to see the vessel; they were only blinded by the glare.

Captain Daniels scarcely looked up; he seemed paralysed.

A few minutes and the moon shone out clear and bright, and by her light the vessel could again be plainly seen. Again she had altered her course, and was this time steering straight down upon the boat.

"Hurrah!" The shout burst involuntarily from the men, and Captain Daniels, half dazed, looked up. The relief was so great that he hardly dared believe his eyes. Yes, thank God! they had seen the danger, and were trying to avoid it.

Would they succeed? It was hard to say —a few seconds would decide.

Packet after packet of the red-fire powder was lighted and burned without intermission.

Once their ears caught a sound of grinding and scraping, and they groaned as they saw the vessel stagger for a moment, as though she had received a blow. Then a wave passed under her bows, and on it she rode into safety.

The danger passed, Captain Daniels, trembling with anger and indignation, hastened on board to demand an explanation of the foolhardy business, and to give Evans "a piece of his mind."

He was met on the deck by a young seaman.

" Where is Evans ? "

" Captain Evans is ill, sir."

" And who are you ? "

" I am Noel Merrick. The captain is my uncle. I shipped with him in Queenstown as first mate. We have had an accident, but, except the injury to my uncle and the loss of our anchors, no great damage is done."

" No great damage! Do you know how near you came to destruction? What did you mean by taking such a risk? You a stranger ! Where is Evans ? "

The young man's coolness infuriated the old captain.

" He is down below, sir—dying, I think. As to the risk, I did not consider it so great. I know this coast well, and the captain had described this harbour so often that I should not have hesitated to attempt it in daylight."

" Why on earth did you not wait till day-light ? "

" We had no choice, sir, in this gale. Our anchors went some hours ago. I thought we might as well make a try for safety, as be driven on shore like a log."

Captain Daniels was perforce content, though he made a mental note to inquire more fully into the matter at the first opportunity.

Later, in the kitchen of the little brown house, in the presence of the parson, and several of Captain Daniels' particular cronies, Noel Merrick was subjected to a severe cross-examination.

"We have had," he said, "nothing but storms since leaving Queenstown. Two days ago the wind chopped round and blew a gale from the north-east, and we were driven out of our course. A heavy sea was running and the *Martha* made bad weather of it and rolled fearfully. The jolly-boat was displaced from the chocks on the main hatch, and was thrown against the bulwarks; the captain, who could not get out of the way in time, was jambed in between. Several of his ribs seemed broken. He could not speak, and was in great pain. I got him below and did what I could to make him more comfortable, and then I went on deck and took charge.

"Yesterday we sighted the Lizard. The

gale did not abate, but the wind chopped and changed, then settled down to the southwest and blew a strong gale. We had lost both anchors. The sea was very heavy, and the brig laboured fearfully. The captain thought we had better try to lie off till daylight, but he was very bad, and I thought he would die before morning unless he got help.

"I sighted the Scar before sundown, and tried to make it before dark. The wind was fair, and the brig answered her helm splendidly. I felt sure I could bring her in with the flood tide. All went well, till suddenly I saw a red light flare up straight ahead.

"I got a mortal fright, as I naturally thought it a warning signal. I altered the vessel's course a point or two, but I felt desperately anxious; I had been so sure of the position of the channel, and the red lights put me out of my reckoning. I would have given everything to be able to put back, but it was too late, the wind and tide drove us on.

"I stood at the helm, but I felt utterly helpless. I could only say over and over

again to myself, 'God help us.' Then a
strange thing happened, which I suppose no
one will believe. I heard a voice in my ear,
saying clearly and distinctly, 'Make for the
red fire—steer for the light.'

"I could not see where the voice came
from. It was dark. But as I glanced over
my shoulder, my hand which held the wheel
was grasped and I let go. For a second it
flew round, and when I caught it again, a
small hand laid itself on mine, and I felt
compelled to obey its pressure, and put the
helm hard to starboard.

"'Steer for the light,' said the voice
again, and then I saw the speaker had the
white-clad form of a woman. I obeyed her
words and the pressure of her hand, but
I thought I had lost my senses. I could
think of nothing for a moment, but then I
collected myself and steered for the light.

"The white woman stood beside me,
keeping her hand on mine, and together
we watched how the vessel struggled like
a living thing to obey the helm, and shivered
as she strove against the force of the wind
and waves. She did obey splendidly, but

s

I heard and felt how she grated her keel on the sunken rocks, and I thought all was lost. In that moment the moon broke through the clouds and the light fell on the white figure. I saw it was like a girl with long light hair, and great eyes that were fixed on the red light; a slender, delicate-looking creature; but still, if I had not known it was impossible, I should have taken her for a mortal woman.

"She never looked at me, nor did she speak again, but stood still with her hand on mine, impelling it to keep the vessel heading direct for the flaring red fire. Then, a minute later, I heard the sound of 'Hurrah,' and saw the boat from whence the sound and the light had proceeded. In the same instant the hand lifted from mine, and the figure was gone.

"These are the reasons why the brig's course was altered, and is all I can tell you. Who she was, or where she came from, only God knows, but it was she, not I, who brought the brig into safety."

The explanation was a strange one, and Noel Merrick was subjected to many a cross-examination, but he had only one reply to give. "I can tell you nothing more, it was just as I have said."

But there came a time, and that shortly, when Noel Merrick did have more to tell, though what he said raised the gravest doubts in Captain Daniels' mind as to the wisdom of a promise he had made, to put the young sailor in command of the brig. He had been urged thereto by Gennifer, who had expressed her decided conviction that Noel Merrick was the cleverest sailor, as well as the handsomest and best man, she had ever seen, nobody but her father excepted. Captain Daniels, after a few days' acquaintance with the young man, was disposed to see him with his daughter's eyes, and to congratulate himself on having found so efficient a substitute for the invalided Evans. The awakening came a few days later, when he and the young sailor were returning in the moonlit dusk from a visit to the *Martha*, which was undergoing the needed repairs. As they neared the house a slender white figure came through the doorway into the moonlight to meet them.

"There she is again!" exclaimed the sailor, stopping short.

"She? Who?"

"It was she!" pointing to the approaching girl, "that girl, or angel, or whatever she is, that brought in the brig."

"She! Why, that's Marah."

Marah had been ill. Cold and exposure, and perhaps excitement on the night of the vessel's incoming, had been too much for her delicate frame, and on her recovery from the long, deep fainting fit, she had been obliged to keep her room, so that she had not met the young sailor who was the object of Gennifer's enthusiastic admiration; nor, when she did see him, could she understand the look of wonder, akin to awe, with which he regarded her.

Both girls were puzzled to understand why the father should wish to draw back from his given word; "I could believe in the angel steering the brig," said Captain Daniels confidentially to his wife, as they sat by the fireside discussing matters; "there's more wonderful things than that in the Bible; but when it comes to him a-swearing that the angel was the maid Marah, it's too much; there's no sense nor reason in it, for we know as how it ain't true. I'm sore puzzled in my mind what to do."

But if the captain had a difficulty in making up his mind as to the wisdom of trusting his ship in the young man's hands, his daughter decided without hesitation a much more momentous question; for, before the brig was ready for sea again, Gennifer announced her intention of trusting herself and her future, for better or worse, to him.

She overruled all objections, and had her own way, as she had done all her life, and when pretty Gennifer made up her mind to anything, there was nothing more to be said.

One more voyage, however, Captain Daniels held out for, and then, if all went well, he would not oppose the young people. So Noel Merrick sailed away with the brig, and Gennifer waited at home for him, glad and joyful in the new happiness that had come into her life.

There was so much to do, so much to

prepare, that the time passed quickly. There were letters to receive and read—beautiful letters that made the girl's heart beat, and brought the bright colour to her cheek. There were letters to write too, that brought a softer beam to the bright dark eyes. In her happiness she did not notice at first the pathetic little droop that was sometimes to be seen on Marah's face, nor the wistfulness that had come into her eyes. It was only when the neighbours remarked that the girl was failing, that she saw her step had lost its lightness, and .that her eyes and lips wore an expression they had not known before.

The change had come about slowly. She was not ill, she said, and refused to be treated as an invalid; nevertheless, it was plain to all that she was fading away. She had no pain; she never complained, nor did they see how the weakness increased. It was only when they compared this week with the last, or the present month with the previous one, that they saw the change was both great and rapid.

She strove to hide her weakness, and took

as eager an interest in the preparations for the wedding as did the bride herself. She watched Gennifer's blushing cheeks and love-lit eyes, when she opened and read the closely written pages of her lover's letters, but no one saw the lips quiver, or the hunger in her own eyes, as she listened to the passages the girl would read aloud to her.

The year was nearing its close, and it was plain to the fisher-folk that Marah's life was going with it, but the girl seemed unconscious of her illness.

The *Martha* had started on her homeward voyage. There could be no more letters from Noel Merrick. The new year would bring him with it, and Gennifer had a little bird in her heart that sang and fluttered joyously as she went about her daily tasks and counted the days that brought her lover nearer.

The weeks passed, the time for his return drew nearer—nearer—arrived—and passed, leaving Gennifer bewildered. What could it mean? she asked her father, who answered, "It is nothing, he will come soon." But

the days grew into weeks, the weeks resolved themselves into months, but brought
no news of the ship nor her lover. Each
morning the girl said to herself, "He will
come to-day." Each evening she murmured
with trembling lips, "He will come to-
morrow," but the day passed, and the
morrow came, but Noel did not come with
it. The girl's pretty colour faded, and her
eyes grew like Marah's in their longing and
wistfulness. In all her young life trouble
had never come so near her. Her gladsome
heart had never known a sorrow or bereavement. She seemed unable to understand
that so terrible a grief could befall her; she
thought that she must awake and find it
all a miserable dream.

Marah watched her with pitying looks
which Gennifer could not bear. "Do not
look at me as if you were sorry for me,"
she would say passionately. "It is as if
you had already decided he could never
return. He will come soon; I will not be
pitied."

But he did not come, nor did there come
any news of him. But once a homeward-

bound steamer reported the picking up of fragments of wreck, and on one they found the painted name *Martha*. Then the conviction was forced upon the old people and the fisher-folk that the brig had gone, and that they had heard the last of Noel Merrick and his men. But Gennifer would not submit; she was not one to bear her sorrow with patience; she resented the cross with all her strong young nature, and fought wildly against the decree of bereavement. She refused to wear a black gown, which would be a sign of her acceptance of the fact that her lover was lost to her.

She was too proud to show despair, though in her heart there was no hope. She held her head high and defiantly before others; only Marah knew of the sleepless nights, and restless tossings on the couch, from which the girl would rise with miserable eyes and aching head.

And all this time Marah was slipping quietly out of life. Little by little she had relinquished her daily tasks into Gennifer's hands—chiefly, it seemed, because she saw the girl needed fuller occupation for her fingers during the weary hours—but, once relinquished, she was not able to take them up again.

As long as her feet would carry her, she would walk along the sands to the boulder of rock, where as a child her baby feet had taken her, and sitting there would dreamily gaze out over the sea as she had done then.

It was there that Gennifer sought her one day, and throwing herself on the sand, hid her face against Marah's knee, and burst into a passion of tears and convulsive sobs that shook her with their violence.

They were the first tears the girl had shed during the miserable months of waiting, and Marah did not try to stem their flow; she only carressed the drooping head, while her eyes softened with an infinite pity for the girl's grief.

"O Marah! I cannot bear it; my heart will break. I could never have believed this would be the end. If I could only die," she moaned, but Marah's hand only lingered caressingly on her hair; she did not speak.

By-and-by the sobs and moans died

away, and the girl lay still, exhausted by the storm. Then she remembered that the evening air was chill, and Marah must come home. She rose to her feet saying, "Come, let us go," when the sight of the younger girl's face startled her. A bright, eager, wondering expression was spread over the pale delicate features, and the wide-open blue eyes shone with a glad light. Over the parted lips a smile, half incredulous, wholly delighted, played. She rose eagerly to her feet, and stretching out her arms seemed as though about to throw herself into the approaching waves.

"What is it? Marah, what is it?" cried Gennifer; but she did not hear.

"Noel! Noel!" The name broke from the parted lips as though forced from them by surprise and wondering joy.

Gennifer threw her arms around her, as the girl, with a look of joy and happiness, fell pale and inert at her feet.

"O Marah, what did you see? It was not his ghost? He is not dead? Do not tell me that? Oh, what shall I do! She is dying!" Gennifer's cries brought speedy help, and the fainting girl was carried to her home. In a little while, she opened her eyes and gazed with the same glad smile at Gennifer's anxious, tear-swollen face.

"You were right, Gennifer; he is not dead, for I have seen him."

"Tell me, dear! What did you think you saw out there on the sands? You frightened me so, I was afraid you were dying."

Marah patted her hand softly, still smiling. "I see many things away over the sea— strange, beautiful things sometimes, but this was different. It seemed to me that an island rose up out of the sea, and came towards me. It was as if all else was dark, and all the light lay on the island and round about. The sea grew more blue, and more still; the skies more clear and bright; the sunshine, stronger and warmer, glittered on the waters and on the white sands. There were many strange trees and brilliant flowers, such as I have never seen before, and the air was laden with soft perfumes. There were people too—men and women—with brown skins, and wearing but little clothing. They laughed and talked to each other. There were other people there, wearing different clothing; they were white men—I counted nine of them. They could not talk to the dark people, but made signs, and the others laughed, and laughed so loud that I heard them plainly. There was some one else in what I think was a garden, or perhaps only among some flowering shrubs. He heard them too and came out, and as he came from among the leaves I saw it was Noel. I could hardly believe it; I had not thought of him though the other white men had seemed a little familiar. Then he laughed a little at something he saw—which had made the others laugh—and then I knew I was not mistaken, and I cried out 'Noel! Noel!' He heard me, I think, for he started and looked round. But then the island, the people, the green trees, the sparkling blue calm waters vanished, and all was dark. I felt myself falling, and heard your voice in my ears, and then—when I awakened I was here."

"If it were only true, instead of just a dream, O Marah, how happy I should be."

"Dear, it is true! I know it is true. You may believe me, Gennifer. I do not know where the brig is; I do not know where that island is; but I know that wherever it may be, Noel is alive and is on it, and all the others with him. You need not weep for him again, Gennifer; he will come back to you." And Gennifer believed.

After this the girl failed rapidly. She could no longer wander down to the sea, and soon she could not rise from her couch, but lay where she could watch the sunlit waves through the open doorway, with a look of wistful longing in the soft blue eyes.

"He will come, Gennifer; I know he will come, but I begin to fear I shall be gone. You will be very happy, Gennifer; you will be good to him because you love him." And Gennifer could only weep, but they were not despairing tears such as she had shed down on the seashore, but soft pitying tears for the fair young life that began in sorrow, and was, she felt—though no word had said it— closing in disappointment, and she wondered a little what she had done to merit the happiness she felt sure would be hers; while

Marah, the pure, the gentle, was sinking into her grave unblessed by that which had filled her own life with promise.

The grass had not yet grown over Marah's resting-place in the churchyard overlooking the sea, when he came. The story he told was read by the world. Of how the *Martha* had foundered away in the southern seas. Of how the men and he spent many days in a small boat, trying to reach land, and how at last they succeeded. Of how they reached an island whose inhabitants received them kindly, and with whom they stayed many weeks, till a passing vessel carried them off to a frequented port, where they found a ship to bring them home. They had come by the same vessel which carried their letters, so that they were themselves the bearers of the news.

It was no uncommon story, but when they told Noel of Marah's vision, which had brought so much comfort and strength to Gennifer's breaking heart, he said, "It was no dream. It was all as she said. I heard a glad voice crying 'Noel! Noel!' and I knew it was the voice of the angel who had said, 'Steer for the light,' and the angel, I knew, was Marah."

In after years when the fishers of Pentraginny placed lights on the buoys which now mark the entrance to their little harbour, they called one "Martha" and the other "The Angel," and round the buoy, in great white letters—which in daylight may be read by sailors on the sea outside—they painted the words "Steer for the light!"

THE END

Printed by BALLANTYNE, HANSON & CO.
Edinburgh & London